PRAISE FOR S.T. GIBSON

ODD SPIRITS

S.T. GIBSON

ANGRY
ROBOT

ANGRY ROBOT
An imprint of Watkins Media Ltd

Unit 11, Shepperton House
89-93 Shepperton Road
London N1 3DF
UK

angryrobotbooks.com
twitter.com/angryrobotbooks
Who you gonna call?

An Angry Robot hardback original, 2024

Edited by Eleanor Teasdale
Cover by Alice Claire Coleman
Illustrations by Eleonor Piteria
Tarot Card descriptions by Adam Gordon
Set in Meridien

ISBN 978 1 91599 859 0
Ebook ISBN 978 1 91599 860 6

Printed and bound in the United Kingdom by CPI Group (UK) Ltd, Croydon CR0 4YY.

9 8 7 6 5 4 3 2 1

To everyone who helps me believe that love is enough, even on days when that belief is hard-won.

CHAPTER ONE

RHYS

Rhys had been the first to notice. He wasn't initially sure whether the small household items that went missing were anything to be concerned about, so he wrote it off as mere forgetfulness. For a week, he tolerated not being able to find the scissors, or his favorite necktie, or his car keys. He consigned himself to slapping sticky note reminders onto his laptop to try to prevent himself from mislaying things. He even managed to brush off the night he woke up feeling positive that something was in the bedroom, lingering just out of sight. In his line of work, you had to have a strong stomach for the uncanny.

Rhys was too intimately acquainted with the unseen world to jump at shadows. He did not consider himself a superstitious man. But he was anxious, and his anxiety made him overly aware of every little detail out of place.

It was probably nothing.

It wasn't until he opened the door to his study to find

every single book removed from the shelves and arranged into tottering stacks on the floor that Rhys resolved to take the matter up with his wife. Rhys hadn't mentioned the strange occurrences to her, hoping that she might be the first one to bring it up, or that he was hallucinating the whole thing. But now, he needed her expertise. She had always been the more even-keeled one in their marriage, as a person and as an occultist.

"You can't be serious," Moira said with a little laugh. She was tending a pot of chamomile and calendula simmering on the stove, and the billowing steam gave her skin a fresh-from-the-sauna glow. Little baggies of spices and bundles of dried herbs were spread across the counter in an explosion of color. The kitchen was the warmest room in the house, and so made an excellent makeshift greenhouse for Moira's potted yarrow, five finger grass, and high john. When Rhys had stepped through the kitchen door, their leaves had given a little shiver as though they were happy to see him.

"Don't tell me you haven't noticed weird things happening around the house lately," he said, arching an eyebrow at his wife. *Wife*. It was still thrilling to think, even more thrilling to say. They had only been married for a year, after all. That newlywed buzz made up for any passing tiff.

"Well, yes," she conceded, leaning forward to waft steam towards her nose and inhale deeply. "But I figured it would sort itself out with time. Uncanny things happen every day in this house."

Rhys reached out to touch an adolescent oregano plant that grew with its leaves pressing against the windowpane, seeking the sun. Everything Moira touched seemed to blossom, and despite the dark moods that sometimes passed across her like rainclouds, she was most often distilled sunlight. Rhys found himself seeking her touch more and more in the colder months, when his sullen disposition worsened and his tendency towards misanthropy flared.

"Perhaps," Rhys mused. "You don't think any of your clients tracked in any bad energy?"

"I doubt it. I make everyone smoke cleanse with incense before starting the session."

Rhys cut himself a slice of Moira's freshly baked peach pie and poked at the crust thoughtfully. She was often too busy with her private astrology clients and erratic hours at the vintage clothing store to cook, but when she had the time, she filled the house with the scent of pastry. "You've been doing more dreamwork lately. Have you noticed anything strange in the astral?"

"Nope."

"And there's no chance a spirit might have hitchhiked back into our world?"

Moira huffed, sorting through the various items stuck into her up-do in search of a pen. She plucked some sprigs of freesia out of her hair before Rhys reached out to retrieve the ballpoint pen that was securing the hair at the nape of her neck.

"I'm a responsible astral traveler," Moira said. "It's not like I just wander around in limbo saying hello to any spirit that wanders by. Besides, you know I don't even like working with spirits; that's your thing. How can you be sure you didn't forget to properly close down a summoning circle or something like that? You've told me yourself that if you don't formally send a spirit on their way after you summon them, they're liable to stick around."

Rhys was willing to concede that it was possible, but he didn't think it was likely. He had an obsessive attention to detail that often felt more like a curse than a blessing, and he was in the habit of triple-checking his notes after every summoning to make sure he had tied up every loose end.

"I summon under very strict parameters," Rhys said. "I chalk out the proper circle, I bind the spirit with divine names, I make my petition, and then I send them packing and close the circle down."

"And that's never backfired, then?" she said in her sweet, cutting Southern drawl.

Rhys shrugged one shoulder noncommittally. It may be true that unruly demons had trapped Rhys in his study for hours before by jamming the lock on the door, or that he had, in his younger years, occasionally summoned something way above his paygrade that had scared the daylights out of him.

"Maybe once or twice. But not in a long time."

"It's probably just some negative energy passing through," Moira said. "Or an old resident of the house pitching a fit about our renovations to the master bedroom."

"But the house isn't haunted. We had it tested, remember?"

Moira clicked her pen and marked something down in the margins of her recipe book. At least, Rhys thought it was a recipe book. Moira threw her recipes, astrological calculations, financial records, and notes on herbal medicine into the same dingy composition notebook. Rhys kept all of his esoteric research in meticulously labeled encrypted files on his laptop and wrote down summoning notes by hand in his diary, and he never understood how his wife ever found what she was looking for. But then again, Moira's system worked for her, some days better than Rhys's worked for him.

She was the one who was running a profitable supernatural services business out of their home, after all, and Rhys was the one struggling to advance in his own studies.

"I remember," she said. "It was David's wedding present to us."

Her tone was civil, but there was a tightness around her mouth that Rhys was attuned to. She was faintly irritated by the memory of David Aristarkhov, Rhys's oldest friend and a more than serviceable psychic, sweeping through the newly-rented townhouse in search of ghosts. It was a very David thing to do, to give a "present" that was in fact an excuse to grandstand in the spotlight. If Rhys had found the stunt slightly off-color, it had cemented David in Moira's mind as someone who acted in consistently poor taste.

"I could ask around at the Society. See if anyone has ever dealt with something similar?" Rhys asked.

"Respectfully, I'll decline," Moira replied. "I don't need a coven of boys to come in and meddle in my affairs."

"It's not a coven," Rhys said, painfully aware that they were edging up on a sensitive topic. But he couldn't resist the impulse to correct, even when Moira rolled her eyes.

"Everyone's always gossiping about each other and arguing about whether or not to buy new robes," Moira said. "I know a coven when I see one."

Rhys opened his mouth to steer their chat into safer waters, but Moira beat him to it.

"I'm sure it will sort itself out," Moira said, putting a pin in the conversation. This was her usual response to any topic of conversation she didn't like, a sweet smile and a stonewall. "Grab me the honey, will you, baby?"

Rhys rummaged around in the cupboard above the sink for the ceramic jar of Appalachian sourwood honey.

Her ingredients were much better organized than her recipes, with allocated shelves for dry herbs, essential oils, prepared tinctures, and so on.

Rhys sidled up beside his wife and kissed her shoulder as she took the jar from him. Her brown skin was warm under his lips, and she smelled like her signature rose and sandalwood perfume.

"What are you brewing up over there?" he asked, carefully pleasant. He felt like they were dancing close to a disagreement, and he wanted to avoid that at all costs. Married life was bliss, but it had its challenges as well. He and Moira hadn't lived together for very long before getting hitched and moving into the townhouse in Jamaica Plain, and they were still getting used to each other. Ironing out routines, building communication strategies, and bumping into each other's emotional furniture, as his mother might say. They were both incredibly independent people, with strongly articulated personalities. Disagreements were bound to happen.

"That's just a facial toner. But this…" She dribbled the honey over a collection of herbs layered atop each other in a small mason jar. "Is for Ms Rivkin, the librarian. Her future father-in-law is being mean to her, and I figure this ought to sweeten his disposition up before the wedding."

"So you just… give it to her? Or to the father-in-law? How does this sort of operation… operate?"

"Well first of all, in my tradition we call it a spell," she said, slowly, like she was talking to a child. Her tone was indulgent, affectionate even, but Rhys prickled all the same. He hated feeling that there was anything in the universe he couldn't research, catalog, and neatly integrate into his worldview, but Moira's particular brand of magic was still slippery to him. It didn't help that she tended to shrug off his inquiries into her practice, as though drawing a veil between them.

"I know a spell from a ceremonial operation," Rhys said.

"Spells come in all shapes and sizes," Moira went on. "But they all work the same way: I bring together the proper energies and symbols, I infuse them with my intent, and then I give them to the client with instructions about how to bring their conscious and subconscious mind into alignment with that intent."

He watched his wife layer more cut flowers and honey into the jar and nodded along, even though he still wasn't quite sure about the particularities of the whole thing. He was a student of Western esotericism, with its book-learning and ironclad rules. Moira came from a folk magic tradition, one built on faithfully-preserved knowledge passed down through oral traditions and verified with homebrewed trial-and-error. He was a sorcerer, and she was a witch, simple as that. Maybe there were some things they would simply never understand about each other. Some days that impasse saddened Rhys, and he wondered if Moira felt that sadness as well, but since he wasn't sure how to cross that gulf between them, he buried the emotion and soldiered on ahead. He was Irish Catholic; he was good at that.

Still, he should try harder. For Moira. For both of them.

"That all sounds very involved," Rhys said, suddenly feeling stiff and awkward, like he had forgotten how to talk to his greatest love. He was trying to be supportive, but he had a hard time finding the right words. Often, he found himself reliving conversations hours or days after they happened, only then stumbling upon the thing he should have said. "I'm sure you know what you're doing."

Moira's shoulders sagged as she put her final touches
on the concoction, and Rhys wasn't sure if it was because
she was tired from her work or because something had
upset her. So he took her gently by the wrist and kissed
the tips of her fingers, suckling off sweetness where he
found it.

"Did you ask for payment, miss witch?" he said. Business
was familiar to him, and he never shirked from talk of money
or negotiations. Part of the reason he loved Moira was
her canny eye for personal branding and client retention,
although he did sometimes wish she charged loftier rates.
Her services were more than worth it.

Moira scoffed in the back of her throat.

"It's a small spell; it hardly takes any time at all." She
dropped a lock of hair tied with blue thread into the
jar, then screwed the lid shut tightly. "You know I hate
imposing."

"When are you going to let me make you a website?"

"That just feels so... inauthentic. Like I'm trying to sell
people something."

Rhys chuckled. "Love, you *are* selling something."

Moira brushed her cheek against Rhys's then nipped him
lightly on the nose. He was so surprised by the little flash of
ferocity that he blushed, making Moira giggle.

"And selling a service without making folks feel like it's a
transaction is part of the slight-of-hand. It's all a magic trick.
Besides, I prefer to find my clients the old-fashioned way.
Word of mouth and elbow grease. If you worked with the
public, you might have a better understanding."

Rhys tried not to interpret that last bit as a jab. Yes, he
was retiring and reclusive by nature, but Moira didn't have
to point it out.

"Oh yeah?" he said, arching an eyebrow. "You're going around casting spells on everyone by fluttering those butterfly lashes and lending a sympathetic ear?"

"Sympathy is my specialty. Always has been."

"Then how can I be sure you aren't working magic on me?" he asked, brushing his fingertips across her elbow. Moira's eyes flickered over him, dark and warm like a summer night.

"You can't," she said, then drifted out of his reach with a smirk painted on her lips.

"Suit yourself," he said, returning to his untouched slice of pie. When he took a bite, he turned pallid. The plate clattered against the countertop as Rhys set it down and pushed it away.

"What's wrong?" Moira asked.

"It's gone bad," Rhys said, spitting delicately into a nearby trash can. "The peaches taste rotten."

Moira's eyebrows shot up. "That's impossible; I got those at the farmer's market yesterday. They were perfect."

She plucked up Rhys's fork and took a bite, then promptly spit it out as though exorcising herself of something wicked. Displeasure knotted up her mouth as she worked the last of the rancid taste out from between her teeth with her tongue.

"Okay…" she conceded. "That's very weird."

"Nothing more than negative energy, huh?" Rhys needled.

Moira sniffed, then turned to slap a canning label on the completed spell jar. "It's just bad vibrations or something. Open a window and let some air in. It'll pass."

The High priestess

CHAPTER TWO

MOIRA

The intruder went largely uncommented-on for the next few days, but things weren't getting any better. In fact, two otherwise secure paintings crashed to the ground of their own accord, and Moira was once roused from sleep by mysterious nighttime knockings. It wasn't uncommon for the doorbell to ring in the wee hours with someone on the other side sobbing for a tarot reading, a charm bag, some advice, *anything*. Moira always let them in, much to Rhys's sleep-deprived chagrin. He would rather she accept clients by appointment only, but her mother and grandmother had instilled in her a strong community responsibility from a young age, and she always answered the door. Always.

This time, however, she pulled on her robe and hurried downstairs, straightening her spine and gathering her power with a few deep breaths… only to find that no one was outside.

Moira stood on the stoop, blinking in the dark. She felt very cold all of a sudden, and very exposed. With a huff, she wrapped her robe tighter around her, headed back up the stairs, and crawled into bed next to Rhys.

"Who was it?" he asked, voice muffled by the pillow and drowsiness.

"No one," she said, staring up sleeplessly at the ceiling. "Just some neighborhood kids playing ding-dong ditch."

She hoped that perhaps, if she said it out loud, she would believe it. The alternative, that her domestic bliss was being encroached upon by some unseen adversary, was much more unsettling. Moira preached against prosperity gospel and unfettered manifestation mindset every chance she got: it was a machination to make the downtrodden feel guilty for their condition and to encourage the well-off to pat themselves on the back for their piety. But it was so hard not to internalize, on some level, that if something was amiss in her life, it was because she had done something to deserve it. Or worse, because she secretly wanted it.

Moira hoped, in her heart of hearts, that Rhys would ask some sort of follow-up question. Perhaps, with him by her side, she would be brave enough to face reality.

"Damn kids," he murmured, then rolled over and fell back asleep.

Moira sighed, quietly, so Rhys wouldn't hear. She and Rhys had gotten married in the throes of their honeymoon period, and as a result, they didn't have a wealth of experience navigating conflict together. As it stood, when they disagreed, Rhys would disassociate in a book and Moira would fume on the phone to a friend until the couple got tired of being mad at each other. But as far as overcoming obstacles went, they had faced very little worse than the occasional flat tire together. Despite all their spiritual skills, she worried they simply weren't equipped to deal with something like this.

About a week after the disturbances began, Moira was unwinding in the bath with a smutty romance novel and mugwort cigarette. As a general rule, she detested smoking, but she made occasional exceptions for her own herbal blends, targeted towards calming her nerves and sharpening her psychic senses. She needed a little extra grounding after a week of jumping at shadows and trying to ignore the mounting feeling that she was being haunted in her own home. Lo-fi droned on a comforting loop from her phone speaker, which had been propped up on the sill of the cracked window.

Just as the small-town florist in her book was about to get down and dirty with a rival shopkeeper, the faucet let out a concerning rattle.

Moira toed the knob tighter with her foot and returned to her novel.

The faucet rattled again, this time paired with a groan from the piping.

"What in the blue blazes?" Moira muttered, abandoning her dog-eared book at her side. She had a tendency to re-read her favorite love stories when she was feeling particularly stressed. The predictability of a well-worn happily ever after was soothing, and God knew she needed a little extra soothing these days.

Moira pushed up in her rose petal-strewn bath and smacked the faucet with her hand. For a long moment, there was silence. Then, with an unmistakable clarity that made her stomach sink, a thin hissing sound emanated from the tap.

It didn't sound metallic, and it didn't sound mechanical. It sounded like a snake, or worse, like a disembodied person jeering at her through their teeth.

Moira froze for an agonizingly long moment, her pulse pounding in her ears as the water around her went cold. There was no mistaking the sound as a mugwort-induced hallucination, and she trusted her own senses too much to suppose she was imagining things.

The sound sputtered, so very close to a snicker.

Moira was out of the bath in a flash. She didn't bother blowing out the candles on the sink or retrieving her phone from the sill. She just wrapped herself in the nearest towel and slammed the door behind her.

It took a lot to shake her, and even more to scare her down to her bones, and Moira knew that when she was spooked, she could lash out like a frightened child. But that knowledge didn't change the fact that there was only one obvious explanation for her plight, and it was one she was suddenly very fed up with dancing around.

Moira padded down the stairs and bumped the door to Rhys's study open with her hip without knocking.

"Rhys," she said firmly. No endearment, no sweetness. A command.

Rhys looked up from the research he was doing at his desk, one hand tousled in his dark curls that always wanted for trimming. When he saw Moira's state of undress he pushed his charts of planetary hours away.

"You're wet," he said. A groundbreaking observation that did nothing to improve Moira's outlook on the situation. "Is everything alright?"

"I've come to pick a bone," Moira said. She was dimly aware she was dripping all over the elaborate pentagram

Rhys had drawn onto the hardwood with some chalk and the straight edge of a Latin primer, but she didn't much care. She started pacing, trailing water and her bad mood across the study. "I need to talk to you. Now."

Rhys leaned back in his leather chair, the one he had lifted from the dean's office at the university when the old man retired.

"I'm following," he said cautiously.

"I can't even take a bath in peace without some weird shit happening. I'm racking my brain wondering how this could have happened. How could something so *nasty* have gotten into my house, especially after all the warding and cleansing we do? And then I remember. My husband thinks it's fun to call up demons for casual chit-chats."

Rhys kneaded his temples with the tips of his fingers. His affect swung from concerned to intellectualizing on a dime, which only peeved Moira more. He *always* did this when confronted.

"We've been over this, Moira, they aren't demons. Not demons in a classical sense, anyway."

"I don't want to argue semantics with you. Demons, spirits, it makes no difference. I've told you summoning circles are dangerous, and I've asked you to be more careful."

She could feel it, her anger rising. It made her voice thin and grating.

"A summoning circle, when well-cast and properly closed, is perfectly safe," Rhys said.

It was at that moment the portrait on the wall behind him began to weep blood. Moira stood stock still for a moment, frozen by horror, and she gave her husband a withering glance.

"What part of coercing spirits into telling you cosmic secrets is safe?"

Rhys opened his mouth to protest, but Moira cut him off by pointing at the portrait. Rhys turned and started at the sight, then quickly composed himself and began to fastidiously dab at the possessed portrait with a tissue. The blood dribbled down past his fingers onto the rug and congealed into a tacky stain. If Moira had not been busy being mad at her husband, she might have been impressed with the quality of the manifestation.

"The methods I use have been painstakingly researched and recorded in the Goetia," Rhys huffed, distracting himself with the mess so he wouldn't have to look at his wife. This was one of the more irritating things about Rhys: his tendency to choose the route of passive-aggression. Moira would just rather have the fight and get it over with. "By observing proper procedure when I call and bind them, I can question them without putting myself at risk. I told you when I met you; this is what my magical practice looks like. You said you were fine with it."

Moira watched the delicate red rivulets trickle down the old poet's face, reproduced from an original done in oils. Very little of Rhys's study was authentically vintage – they couldn't afford that quite yet – but he took pains to make it appear as though it was.

"I wish you could just do your research on Wikipedia like the rest of us," Moira said, suddenly feeling tired. Perhaps she was being unfair. Or perhaps Rhys was being an ass. And maybe two things could be true at once.

Rhys, a research librarian to the core, pressed a hand over his heart as though affronted by the suggestion that Wikipedia was a valid academic source. He gave up on his attempt to salvage the painting and tossed the tissue down on his desk.

"The spirits have been around since before recorded history. They know more about the universe than *Wikipedia* does."

A sickly chill swept through the room, causing Moira to draw her towel tighter around herself.

"Listen," she said. "I don't care what you do with your friends at your secret society meetings, but I've made it clear I don't like you bringing it home with you."

Rhys sighed, the fight falling from his shoulders, and crossed the room. He reached out to touch her, perhaps to wrap her in his arms, to wipe the cold droplets of bathwater from her clammy skin, but Moira hunched her shoulders, warding him off. He had already made her mad, and as a matter of fact, Rhys had been irritating her more and more lately. Traits she had found charming when they were dating had become pet peeves after their race to the altar, and she was trying to square her guilt over that fact with the image of Rhys she had built up in her head.

Falling in love had been easy, so she assumed married life would be as well. From where she was standing now, that previous belief illuminated nothing more than her naiveté.

Getting engaged had draped her in a faultless glow. It had added a certain charm to even her worst habits. When Moira was a fiancée, her flightiness had been quirky, her lust for life had been exciting, and her refusal to turn down any adventure had made her leading lady material. But now, as nothing more than a wife, the future stretched out in front of her in an endless sprawl of Hallmark card tedium.

Most women would be satisfied with sweet. They would seek out stability. But, in the most secret parts of her heart on the worst of days, Moira worried she was nothing like most women. She worried she wasn't the marrying type after all.

"Moira, let me hold you," Rhys said, as gentle as she had ever heard him. "Let's find you some warm clothes, okay? Come here, love. You're shivering."

Moira wanted to relent. She wanted to bury her face in his chest and breathe in the scent of his skin and herbal aftershave. But it was so hard to talk herself down from these big emotions when they seized her.

"Moira," Rhys said, somehow even softer. "Please, little goddess."

To Moira's great shame, she found herself blinking back tears. She didn't want to be looked at right now. Not like this. Not when all her faults were on full display, and not when Rhys' own failings would only chafe against her heart until she was, terribly and inevitably, sick even of his kindness.

"I want you to do whatever ceremonial shit it takes to fix this, Rhys," she said, looking past him to the stained portrait. "I'm serious."

Rhys's hand dropped from the air, and he scowled down at his shoes. He worked at the inside of his cheek with his teeth for a moment, then nodded. When he looked back at her, his eyes were hard and clear. The man she woke up next to in the morning had disappeared. Only the sorcerer remained.

"I'm telling you I didn't do this," he said. "When I call something up, I send it away when I'm done; it doesn't stick around and bang my cupboards at all hours of the night. Besides, most of the spirits I summon are perfectly civil. It's a mutually beneficial arrangement."

Moira just shook her head and padded towards the door. If she stayed in the room a moment longer, she feared they would find themselves in the middle of a proper fight.

"Whatever arrangement you have with this thing," she called over her shoulder, "end it."

The High priestess

CHAPTER THREE

MOIRA

In the beginning, all their differences had felt divinely ordained, like the universe had conspired to bring together two polar opposites into loving union. Even the circumstances of their meeting had felt fated.

Moira had just finished her junior year at the Rhode Island School of Design the summer she met Rhys. She often took day trips out of Providence towards Boston to procure spiritual supplies for her dorm room rituals. Even though Salem was a buffet of metaphysical shops, Moira often found herself priced out of their wares, and she didn't enjoy sifting through all the culturally appropriative white sage, lab-dyed crystals, and whitewashed occult books to find what she was looking for. So, on a student budget and with ironclad determination not to water down her family traditions for the sake of convenience, she got creative.

Moira's usual shopping route took her through Jamaica Plain, one of Boston's southernmost neighborhoods, to her favorite gem store, gardening center, and stationary shop in order to meet her varied needs.

Moira began to notice the same man while running her errands: sharply dressed and inevitably reading long and precise lists of necessities off his phone to the shopkeeper. She sometimes stole a glance at him while she was buying her selenite or packets of yarrow seeds, just long enough to catch him holding a crystal sphere up to the light or signing a request order for sheaf parchment. Moira had always found something about his focused air captivating. Until she got stuck behind him in line at the candle boutique with three heavy beeswax candles balanced in her arms.

"I'm sorry, but they all have to be exactly the same size," the strange man told the cashier. "Twelve inches."

She peered around the stranger's shoulder to find him comparing two white taper candles by balancing them both upright on the counter.

"I can trim the longer ones, but shorter ones won't do," he fretted. "Listen, I'm awfully sorry but do you have a tape measure? I forgot mine at home."

The shopkeeper muttered something and began rummaging around behind the counter. Moira set her candles on the ground with a clatter and let out a sigh.

She had a feeling she was going to be in line for a while.

Moira watched quietly as the man measured each candle before allowing the cashier to bag them. Once she accepted the delay, her irritation faded into curiosity. This stranger had beautiful, long-fingered hands, but his nails were dirty with charcoal or ash. His face was angular and short, giving him a boyish quality despite his pronounced cheekbones and the dark circles under his eyes. He looked like he hadn't slept well for a long time, and there was a smudge of white chalk on his elbow.

A sorcerer if she had ever seen one.

She breathed in, second-guessing herself until the last possible moment when she said,

"I doubt a stray centimeter is going to ruin any ceremony worth its salt."

The man turned to scan her face with black eyes. His gaze was unscrupulous, but Moira stood her ground in her platform sandals and stared right back. He had that look; arresting and incisive with something velvet-soft just under the surface.

Magician's eye, her mother always called it.

Finally, Rhys turned away from her and said, "Details matter. God and the devil and all that."

"Well, here's hoping one of them shows up," Moira quipped back.

A smile touched his mouth briefly before darting away. There was something unspeakably satisfying about getting him to crack a smile. She couldn't recall ever having seen his stony countenance soften before.

"That's the idea," Rhys said. He nodded down towards the candles at her feet. "Are those for Litha?"

She smirked, pleased with their little guessing game. Litha was a witches' sabbat, one of six seasonal holidays celebrated by Wiccans in particular, and earth-centered spiritualists widely. Moira wasn't Wiccan: she was barely Baptist on a good day, and she didn't wholeheartedly subscribe to any one religious tradition at all. In her family, they just called the holiday the summer solstice, but she would give him partial credit for his guess.

"Solstice prep waits for no one. Are you Wiccan?" she asked.

Rhys noticed that the cashier was watching them, and he deftly swiped his credit card, plucked up his bags, and turned to leave.

"Ah, no. I'm a bit more of a traditionalist."

"Oh." She tugged at the hook on her overalls for a minute, not sure how to proceed. "Well. Nice to meet you."

Rhys smiled cordially and slipped by, and Moira thought that was the last she was likely to see of him. But then he touched her lightly on the wrist as he passed and leaned down and said, "Enjoy the solstice."

Moira smelled rosemary and vetiver, and suddenly her face felt hot. Before she could say anything else, he was gone, the bell on the door dinging behind him. She watched through the shop windows as he unlocked the driver's side door to a battered gunmetal Lincoln parked on the street. A Williams College sticker was displayed proudly in the back window, and a rosary hung from the rearview mirror.

The cashier cleared his throat.

Moira tore her eyes away from the car and gave a bashful smile.

"Receipt, please," she said.

The weeping paintings and malfunctioning plumbing continued as the days progressed. When Rhys went off to work, Moira was often overcome by a creeping sensation that she wasn't alone in the house. Her anxiety was only worsened by the onset of autumn, which meant that her hours at the vintage store would dwindle and Rhys's schedule as a special collections librarian at the university would be full to bursting. While her husband had his hands full with freshman seminars on proper research technique and back-to-back viewing sessions for faculty who just *had* to examine their illuminated manuscripts before week's end, she was followed around her house by her growing sense of unease. Sometimes this sense was accompanied by the faint scuffling of footsteps that vanished as soon as she whirled to face them.

Moira started making long lunch dates with her friends to keep herself out of the house, and encouraged her clients to meet her at local cafés for tarot readings instead of at her kitchen table. Her old girls' group from RISD wanted to know everything about her married life, and she danced around their questions with smiles and platitudes. She was deliriously happy, she told them, knowing privately that there was simply no other option.

No matter that she sometimes felt, at barely twenty-four, that she might have jumped into marriage too early. So many of the textile artists and indie fashion designers she had buddied up with in college had colorful sex lives and dated all kinds of interesting people, sometimes more than one interesting person at a time. Ginger and her boyfriend were exploring tantric sex together. Amari had blossomed into her quarter-life lesbianism and was being courted by an older woman who worshipped her utterly, not to mention paid for everything. And, after swearing off dating for a whole year, Chava had met someone volunteering who had introduced her to solo polyamory, and now she was thriving in multiple romantic entanglements.

Could that have been Moira's life, if she had chosen a different path?

She tried not to dwell on this question when she let herself in the back door in the evenings (the front door had recently developed a penchant for locking her out), or when she tried to breathe through her nightly yoga sessions. She tried not to get frustrated when her attempts to divine the answer to their troubles with tarot cards turned up nothing but reversals and nonsensical spreads, or when her sprinkle of protective herbs in the four corners of the house proved similarly ineffectual. She tried not to notice that the more tired and skittish she became, the more absorbed Rhys became in his studies. It wasn't uncommon for her husband to devote hours a day to his private study of ceremonial magic, the antiquated kind that required proficiency in Biblical Hebrew and medieval German. But his book binges and research fixations had only increased in the wake of their uninvited house guest, and sometimes she wouldn't see him until they met up to go to bed. She was aware that she might be able to patch things up if she just made herself vulnerable, if she just opened her arms to him and asked for the comfort she ached for. But vulnerability was scary, and opening up was hard, so she busied herself with client work and hobbies instead. Rhys would come around eventually, and the spiritual activity in her house would die down with time. It had to.

Still, it was impossible not to notice that she and Rhys were slowly but surely drifting apart, as slowly and surely as her house was becoming utterly inhospitable.

The Chariot

CHAPTER FOUR

RHYS

Rhys tossed down his pencil and squeezed the bridge of his nose. He flipped through the book of summoning seals on his desk, skimming over the elaborate designs used to conjure and bind myriad spirits: amiable, nasty, or otherwise. Finding nothing of use, he scowled down at the book.

It had been weeks since the trouble started. Rhys had spent much of that time trying a number of involved rituals to suss out exactly what kind of spirit was wreaking havoc in his home.

He had fasted and abstained from sex in preparation, then consecrated his tools with hyssop, drawn the seals on the ground in obsessive detail, pronounced the Latin perfectly… and nothing happened. No meddling spirit manifested for him to bind, and the hauntings continued. He had dredged all the spell books on his shelves for the answer, and it felt like he had exhausted every ceremonial magic tradition the

Western world had to offer. He had even said a novena to Saint Michael as a last-ditch effort.

Still nothing.

He was intimately aware that his fervent study was only drawing him further away from his wife, but whenever he tried to reach out to her, she seemed distracted and disinterested. He wasn't sure if she was spending more and more time away from the house to get away from the malevolent spirit, or from him, and as much as he tried not to internalize it, it started to feel like a pointed message. It began to feel as though Moira would not be able to summon respect for him if he wasn't able to do his duty (as the *man of the house*, the part of his brain steeped in parochial school teaching thought) and keep their domicile safe.

Rhys was probably projecting, but that wasn't a chance he was willing to take. He wanted to fix things with Moira, and that started with fixing things with the house.

Rhys pressed the heels of his hands to his burning eyes and let out a low groan. Far away, the grandfather clock ticked faithfully, reminding him of the late hour. Moira was probably already asleep. Maybe he should go climb into bed and wrap his arms around her, pull her in for a drowsy kiss. Or maybe, as he had done so many nights before, he would undress quietly and retire to his side of the bed, leaving her to her dreams.

Very close, too close to be imagined, Rhys heard a huff of laughter.

He shot out of his chair and made a beeline for the door, and he was halfway up the stairs before his heart stopped pounding. The back of his neck, Rhys realized, was still burning with cold.

He had felt its icy breath when it laughed. It had been *that* near to him.

A door at the end of the hall beckoned as he paused at the top of the stairs, debating whether he ought to just go to bed to sleep off his unease. In the end, he followed the glow of light under the door to Moira's meditation room.

Mediation struck Rhys as a very honorable and healthy habit he wasn't disciplined enough to pick up, much like praying the rosary. Both practices required him to sit still and surrender to the idea that life was not entirely in his control, and these were two things he avoided at all costs. Still, it helped keep Moira grounded and clear-headed, so there must be something to it.

At first, he could hear nothing through the door, but then her crisp, witch-about-town voice drifted towards him.

"I do twenty- and forty-five-minute energy alignment sessions, with hour-long sessions available for those in need of deeper healing. We can start with twenty minutes if you like, to see if reiki might help you manage your grief."

Rhys quietly let himself into the room. Moira was seated on a crocheted pouf, her phone wedged between her ear and shoulder as she painted her toenails violet.

"Mediumship? Oh no, I don't do that... I can't recommend it in good faith, but if you're looking to get in touch with a family member who's passed on, I can give you the name of a psychic who knows what he's doing... Oh yes, there are boy psychics, believe it or not."

Moira's meditation room would be impractically small for any other use. Just a sliver of space that jutted out from the house and came to a point with large windows on either side. It was only big enough for a couple of cushions on the ground and a low table covered with raw amethyst, rose quartz, and candles set into crystal dishes.

"You ready?" Moira asked her client. She flipped through a nearby address book. "His name is David, and his number is... Oh, last name?"

Moira quizzed her husband with her eyes.

"Aristarkhov," he said, leaning his hip against the doorframe.

"Aristarkhov," Moira repeated, with slightly less practiced pronunciation. Then she rattled off the number. "Of course, pleasure's mine. You let me know how it goes and feel free to reach out if you ever run into any trouble. You too, sugar. Have a blessed day."

Moira tossed her cellphone onto a nearby pillow and popped a blueberry into her mouth from the bowl on the ground beside her. She had gathered her hair into a silk wrap tied with a big bow and her face was illuminated by the moonlight streaming in through the window. Incense plumed docilly on the windowsill next to a potted ficus, and the scent mingled with the eternal scent of wet roses that clung to her skin.

"Hey," she said softly. There was promise in that softness. An opening, if Rhys was willing to take it.

Rhys thought about telling Moira about his scare in the study, then swallowed the impulse. It was embarrassing, and his problem to handle besides. He didn't want to bother her with his fretting until he had a solution in hand.

Rhys lowered himself down on a cushion.

"How are you?" he asked.

"Alright, I guess," she said, in that rote way that told him they were just going through the motions, filling each other in on their days without going much deeper. "Slow week for business."

"Oh, I figured you were slammed with house calls." He swallowed again, summoning his courage. "I haven't seen you much in the last couple of days."

Moira shook her head as she screwed the cap back onto her nail polish. "I did that house blessing last week and that was it. Clients keep slipping through my fingers. So many folks looking for mediums this time of year."

"The holidays are coming up. It's a hard season for anyone who's lost a loved one."

"I just don't like it. You know this."

"I do."

"I feel like it never comes to anything good, dragging people back into the past like that. Not to mention so many psychics are hucksters."

Rhys shrugged. He worried at his thumbnail with his teeth. "Some of them do a lot of good."

"Mm," Moira said, unconvinced. Then, "You're wrecking your nails. Anxious?"

Again, the thought of letting Moira know how afraid he had been, how helpless he was starting to feel, crossed Rhys's mind. Again, he watched it drift out of his reach.

"Frustrated. I'm not getting anywhere with our pest problem."

Moira let out a sigh. She seemed very tired, which wasn't surprising. Rhys could feel her tossing and turning at night, troubled by fitful dreams.

"Baby, I've fumigated this house from top to bottom, burned candles, done a floor wash with Florida water, everything I can think of to send that spirit packing," Moira said. "Do you think we're out of our wheelhouse?"

Her husband said nothing, just continued to gnaw at his damaged cuticles.

"You should let me bring in a prayer team," Moira went on. "You never know, it might help."

"Maybe," Rhys said, but he sounded doubtful.

Moira drifted in and out of religious spaces with an ease Rhys was privately jealous of. She never seemed to feel like a prodigal daughter or like she was obligated to attend services more than it pleased her shifting whims.

Moira had taken Rhys to church with her once, back when they had first started dating. Rhys had been raised in a staunchly Catholic neighborhood in Boston and had never been to a Baptist church before, certainly not one where the congregation prayed over each other in the aisles while the pastor preached extemporaneously. Everyone had been welcoming to him, but Rhys couldn't relax in the easygoing atmosphere. It didn't help that the congregation was largely Black and Rhys, who was not used to being in the minority, felt as though he stood out. He knew full well this discomfort was his to sit with and reflect on, privately. Moira had told him about her countless experiences being overlooked or disrespected in majority white spaces, and he didn't want his own awkwardness to tarnish the community she found at her church. He worried that his brooding presence beside her dampened her sparkle, made it more difficult for her to be herself without worrying about introducing him to everyone. So when Moira had invited him to go back with her, he had politely made up an excuse about wanting to get back into Catholic life. That had been a year ago. He had gone to Mass a grand total of six times since.

"There's always Father Mulligan," Rhys suggested. "He's been leading my parents' parish for thirty years; he's seen it all. He might have some tricks up his sleeve."

"Maybe," Moira said doubtfully.

Moira had gone to Rhys's church one Thanksgiving visit, and to hear her tell it, she had found the smoky solemnity of the Mass off-putting. It was beautiful, of course, but beautiful in the way sixteenth century paintings were: ostentatious, and in a way that clearly communicated they were not to be touched. Even though the priest had smiled at her when she followed Rhys up through the communion line, she told him later she was angry that she wasn't allowed to take the eucharist with him. It certainly didn't help that she didn't see many others who looked like her in the small, deeply Irish congregation. Rhys didn't hold any of this against her, but she had never come back with him, and organized religion had become just another impasse between them.

"There's always the Society," Rhys said, steering the conversation away from church. It never seemed to lead them anywhere good.

Moira rolled her eyes. "Come on Rhys, you know I don't get along with them."

"That's not true," he said gently. "Nathan invited us out on his boat just last month and you had a good time, didn't you?"

"I like Nathan fine. I like his wife Kitty better."

"And Cameron gave us that artisanal gin for Christmas last year. What about Antoni? He's a good guy, and he really enjoyed your company."

"I didn't say they were bad guys," she said, shrugging her shoulder. "It's just... The Society is your thing, and I respect that, but it isn't mine."

Moira slid a blueberry into her mouth, then moved over to kneel where Rhys was sitting and took his hand out of his mouth.

"Come here, worrywart. I'll do your nails."

Rhys wanted to keep talking, but Moira was focused on the task at hand. She began to deftly smooth his nails with a metal file, her heavy lashes shading her cheeks as she worked. Rhys's eyes followed the arc of his wife's face, and the slope of her throat down to the curve of her breasts. Then he frowned.

"Where's your necklace, love?"

Moira's hand jumped to her throat. The golden trinity knot on a delicate chain was the first really expensive gift he had gotten her, despite the fact that he could barely afford it. She hardly ever took it off.

"I must have put it down somewhere," Moira said casually, never meeting his eyes. "I'm sure it will turn up."

"You didn't lose it did you? I can help you look for it."

"Hmm? No, of course not."

Rhys tensed up a bit as she switched to his left hand. She had always been a bad liar.

"If you didn't like it, you could have just told me. I wouldn't have been offended."

"I like it," she insisted, filing a bit more vigorously. "I just don't want to wear it every day is all, sometimes it doesn't go with my outfit."

Rhys sensed she wasn't telling him everything, but he kept quiet as she finished her work. Then, she tossed the file aside and finally looked up at him.

"I should finish up these calls," she said.

"Not going to bed?" he said, keeping his voice light.

"Not yet. There's so much to do. What about you?"

"I should get back to my study," Rhys said, running his thumb across the smoothed nail of his ring finger.

Part of Rhys hoped she would push, just a bit, and least

ask him what was wrong. He knew he could be chilly at times, even to those he was closest to. His mother used to call him a little snake, a cold-blooded thing that needed to be warmed by the light of gentleness before opening up to anyone. Rhys was aware he wasn't always an easy man to live with, but he also knew he would uncoil his defenses for his wife, if she only asked.

But Moira's gaze shuttered as she turned back to her phone, killing the conversation for the time being.

CHAPTER FIVE

RHYS

Rhys spent the two weeks after meeting Moira checking and double-checking his preparations for the planetary alignment, mostly to try to put her out of his mind. He would probably never see her again, and it wasn't worth pining after a total stranger, but to simply be looked at and known, perceived in all his strangeness, was electrifying. He had spent most of his life hiding his occult interests from his parents, from his friends, from his professors, and he had convinced himself that he had gotten good at it. But this woman had sussed him out with a single glance, and she had responded to the darkest corners of his heart with a smirk.

He tried not to obsess over whether she had been flirting with him. He tried not to beat himself up over not getting her name.

He failed on both accounts.

When the day of the alignment finally came, Rhys drove

out into farm country beyond the town limits and parked his car in a nondescript location. Then he trekked a half mile into the woods until he came to two footpaths which crossed one another in the middle of a clearing, buzzing with crickets and open to the early evening sky.

Rhys worked quickly and deftly to prepare, measuring out a perfect circle nine feet in diameter in the center of the crossroads. He carved its circumference into the earth with the blade of his athame. The line protected him by keeping anything ill-meaning or unexpected out of the circle, and he was nothing if not cautious.

He dropped his backpack into the middle of the circle and pulled out a dog-eared paperback of hermetic rituals. It was as thick as a phone book and had been bought at a library book sale when he was sixteen. He had asked the cashier to wrap it in newspaper and then smuggled it up the stairs to his bedroom without his mother asking too many questions. His fingers had trembled as he reverently pulled the cover open. When his father had rapped on the bedroom door to tell him dinner was ready, Rhys had shoved the book into a shoebox on the top shelf of his closet where he kept a pack of menthol Camels and his beat-up Hellblazer comics. Dinner had been tasteless, and he kept losing track of conversation as his mind drifted to the contraband waiting for him in his room. Rhys had been twice as excited to unravel its secrets as he had been when he had begged the parish priest to teach him how to turn wine into blood. He had also been sure he would be in twice the trouble if his parents found out about it.

In the crossroads, Rhys quickly located the page he had bookmarked for the evening and began to transfer the planetary symbols into his own circle, carving them with a steady hand into their proper locations.

He became so engrossed in this task that he didn't notice the truck trundling up the dirt road until he could hear rock music in the distance.

Rhys set his dagger down and rocked back onto his knees, as baffled as he was irritated. Who could possibly be out here in the middle of nowhere?

A pickup truck barreled towards him, kicking up dust, and then it veered off the path and parked at an off-kilter angle a few dozen yards from the crossroads. A woman with kinky black hair tied up with a bandana kicked open the door and stared at Rhys. His heart stuttered, recognizing her even before she plucked off her tortoiseshell sunglasses and narrowed her eyes to make out his features.

The witch from the candle shop.

"Hey!" she yelled, cupping her hands around her mouth. "This is my crossroads!"

Rhys stared, the insect song whirring in his ears as he blinked the sun from his eyes. Time slowed to a crawl around him. This wasn't possible. Moreover, he wasn't prepared. How was he supposed to make normal human conversation with anyone, much less a beautiful young woman, when he hadn't been expecting anyone at all? He needed warning before these kinds of things. Maybe an anxiety pill or two.

Finally, Rhys clambered to his feet and said, "This is public property."

"So's the rest of the woods. I've been doing my work here two years running now; you can find another spot."

She was still shouting. The volume of the electric guitar and Caribbean drumming pumping out of the truck's speakers demanded it.

Rhys sighed, pressing his hands to his hips. "Listen, do you think you could turn that off?"

He asked because he detested shouting, but also because she had a touch of Southern accent he hadn't noticed before that he wanted to hear more of.

Moira turned her Santana album down but not off. A cloud of dust rose around her ankles as she hopped out of her truck. She walked purposefully across the clearing and came to a stop just outside of his circle, then let out a low whistle and said, not unkindly, "Wow, you're into some real ceremonial stuff, aren't you? What are you, the ambassador for the Golden Dawn? A.E. Waite come again or something?" She peered into the book still opened in his hand and raised her eyebrows in appreciation. "You're using the source material, even. Is that Latin? I prefer working in the vernacular, myself, but that's impressive."

Rhys was taken aback by the straightforwardness of this young woman in boxy high-waisted shorts and dirty white Keds. His painstakingly polite nature was nudging him to extend his hand for a proper introduction, but he smothered the instinct down. There wasn't any time for pleasantries.

"Listen, if it's all the same to you I've got –" He glanced at his wristwatch, "– eight minutes to finish setting up for this ritual before Jupiter aligns with Saturn. I'd love nothing more than to chat afterwards, but I'm short on time as it stands."

Moira's eyebrows shot up. "Eight minutes you said?"

"That's right."

She quirked a little smile, equal parts pity and mirth. "Oh, honey."

Rhys looked on bewildered as she circled back around to her truck and let down the tailgate with a clang. Candlewax-stained linen and a corked bottle of golden liquid were pulled from one of the cardboard boxes in the truck bed before she produced a composition notebook. She flipped it open and tilted her face up to survey the sky. Then, as though coming to a conclusion that satisfied her, she turned the open composition book to Rhys.

"Your numbers are off," she said.

Rhys stood there in the overgrown crossroads, mosquitoes nipping at his ankles, and found he could hardly scrape words together.

"What?"

"Alignment isn't for another hour and a half," Moira said, simple as arithmetic, plain as daylight.

Rhys sucked in a purposeful breath and began stalking across the grass to Moira. The back of his neck was burning, either from the late June heat or the embarrassment of being taken off guard in a wrinkled Oxford shirt and chinos stained from kneeling in the dirt. He wished he had been ready for her. He wished he could have brushed his hair, swiped on more deodorant, yanked on a pressed shirt, *anything*.

She handed him the notebook and his eyes darted across her calculations. She had painstakingly handwritten the dates and times of that year's major planetary movements one after another in blue ballpoint pen, on the same page as a scribbled guacamole recipe and doodles of stars.

"You calculated this all by yourself?" Rhys asked.

Moira's eyes hardened. He had offended her, he realized with a lurch in his stomach.

"Believe it or not, you don't need a classics degree to be an astrologer," she said, defenses rising.

His chest tightened. How was it that everything he said when it mattered the most always came out wrong?

"No, no, I didn't mean to imply... I'm just impressed!" He passed the notebook back to her with both hands as though it was something priceless. "I pay someone to do mine. I could never learn how."

"Well," Moira said, her features softening as she pressed her notebook to her chest. Her big brown eyes skittered over his face, as though he was a particularly difficult particle she was trying to translate. "Maybe you should fire your astrologer."

"Maybe I should."

They looked at each other for a moment, a nervous smile playing at Moira's mouth, a pink hue rising in the tips of Rhys's ears. Then, Rhys broke the tension with a laugh.

"Now I feel like an idiot for telling you to clear out. I'm sorry." He turned back towards his abandoned circle and ran his hand sheepishly through his hair. "I guess that gives me an hour and a half to find another crossroads."

"Don't bother," Moira said, plucking up the glass bottle from the back of her truck. She wrapped her shirttail around the cork and screwed it out with a hermetically-sealed hiss. "I've got a better way to kill an hour and a half."

Moira poured a splash of her brew onto the ground, and the summer-dry earth greedily drank in the libation. Rhys watched, transfixed, as she brought the bottle to her mouth, had a swig, and then extended it out to him.

He plucked it from her hands with a boldness that surprised him and took a swallow, swiping his tongue along the rim of the bottle to make sure he didn't miss a drop. Sunshine and clover bloomed in his mouth, sharp and honey-sweet.

Mead.

Moira's lips stretched into a succulent smile. They were unpainted aside from a quick swipe of Chapstick that somehow just made her seem more perfect and more kissable. Rhys pretended not to notice this, just as he pretended not to notice the perfume that clung to her clothes as he moved to stand beside her. She smelled like rain-wet greenery and sultry incense and the unapologetically feminine bloom of rose.

Rhys nodded at the boxes tossed into the back of the pickup and did his best to sound cavalier. If they were stuck together out here, they might as well make the most of it.

Not that he minded one bit.

"What else do you have in the back of this truck?"

CHAPTER SIX

MOIRA

Steam enveloped Moira as she stepped into the waterfall shower. It was the only updated appliance in their historic home, but Moira relished in it. She let out a deep sigh as the water slid over her skin, working the soreness out of her muscles.

Moira had been folding jeans and ringing up customers in the vintage shop all day, then came home just to log more hours in the kitchen whipping up spells-to-order. She wasn't one to skip meals, but she had even forgotten to eat dinner, and she felt keyed-up and wound too tight, like a top spinning out of control.

Moira tapped on her collarbones in a soothing somatic rhythm, willing her breathing to slow.

She had been jumping at shadows for weeks, or perhaps at spirits, depending on how she approached the problem. The spiritual activity in their house waxed and waned, but it never really went away. As difficult as she was to spook, her nerves were starting to shred under the ceaseless assault.

You're alright, she thought. *It's all alright.*

There was a light double tap on the shower door, and Moira started. But then she realized it was only Rhys, outlined through the pebbled glass.

"I didn't leave the oven on again, did I?" she asked.

"No," Rhys said with a chuckle. "I was wondering if you wanted company."

A smile spread across Moira's face, and she pressed her hand to the shower door.

"Get in here."

She was treated to the sight of Rhys stripping off his shirt and kicking off his chinos through the hazy glass. The shower door swung open, and a chill crept over her wet skin, but then Rhys slipped in behind her and she felt warmer than she had in ages. His hands settled on her hips and Moira made a deep contented sound, arching her back like a cat.

"Hi, little goddess," he said, and kissed the nape of her neck. Moira tilted her head back so Rhys could kiss her forehead, and she chuckled as he pressed his naked body against hers and held her tightly. It was a mirror image of how he held her as they slept, his chest against her back, but it was even better, because they were both gloriously awake and skin-to-skin.

"You didn't miss me, did you?" she teased.

"Very much," Rhys said, running his hands up her waist to cup her breasts. Delight spread through Moira from the crown of her head to the tip of her toes, and she put her hands over his and gave a little squeeze.

"I thought you were abstaining from the pleasures of the

flesh in order to elevate your soul's vibration, or something," she said.

"I missed you," he sighed, sounding suddenly very old. "And I don't know what I'm doing when it comes to trying to solve this spirit problem. I don't even know where to start."

"You've been at it for weeks," she said, mindful to tread carefully. This was a sort of opening bid from Rhys, a slow unfurling of defenses that she should treat gently if she wanted to get to the heart of the matter. There was a dozen things she could complain about: his distance, their fracturing communication, the nightmare-riddled nights that made them snipe at each other in the morning. But she decided to proceed with grace. "The downstairs hall reeks from all the frankincense you've been burning. You deserve a break."

"I haven't solved the problem yet," he muttered into her skin, and Moira was afraid that he was doing it again, shutting her out to take all responsibility onto himself like some sort of sacrificial lamb. But then he sighed, and Moira felt him smile against her shoulder. "So. There's no point torturing myself with chastity if there's no spell to prepare for."

Moira turned to face him with a grin, hooking her arms around his neck. The water beat down over them, and Moira felt the tightness in his shoulders melt away under her hands.

"You don't mind me hijacking your shower, do you?" he asked, kissing the corner of her mouth with a mounting urgency.

"Not at all," Moira replied, and practically purred when Rhys ran his hand up her thigh and slipped his fingers between her legs.

Maybe things were turning around. Maybe they were going to be okay.

Then, suddenly, there was the awful sound of shattering glass, and Rhys was gone, out of the shower in a flash.

Moira stood dripping and stunned, shivering from the shock and sudden cold. She peered out of the shower, afraid of what she might see.

Rhys was standing over their bathroom mirror, which had somehow dislodged itself from the wall and shattered into a thousand pieces over the sink. As the steam in the room cleared, Moira saw that a large strip of the bathroom wallpaper had been torn from the sheetrock in the process.

"Fuck," Rhys said, looking completely at a loss as surveyed the destruction. "I can't believe… Fuck."

Moira cut the shower off and grabbed her towel.

"Baby, be careful, please. Here–"

She took a step out of the shower, but Rhys held her back.

"Don't, it's a mess, I don't want you to get cut. I just… Let me just get the broom, please. Don't move."

He tied a towel around his waist and did his best to navigate the crucible of broken shards, then hissed when a small piece punctured his heel. Moira watched helplessly as he pulled the glass from his foot and tossed the bloody object into the sink.

As he slipped out of the room to find Band-Aids and a broom, she sank down to the floor of the shower and tried to soothe herself with another breathing exercise.

No matter how deep she pulled the air into her lungs, the sting in her eyes wouldn't go away.

The tarot card hit the truck bed with a crisp *snick*, and Moira sucked her teeth.

"Seven of swords. You're awfully good at playing a part to get what you want, aren't you?"

They were sitting in the back of her pickup, a high school graduation present from her parents that had been ancient then and was pretty much the living dead now. She had no intention of parting with it until the wheels fell off, however. It was her favorite connection to her family, to the South, to her own sense of freedom.

Muggy twilight darkened around them. Rhys's hands were slick with sweat and the condensation from the bottle of mead as he passed it back to her.

"I don't consider myself dishonest," he said. As polite and evasive as any politician.

"Oh?"

"Just... Image-conscious, I guess. I like to make the right impressions."

Moira took a swig. They were sitting cross-legged on a blanket she had produced from under the passenger seat, with Moira's black velvet bag of tarot cards tossed between them. Rhys had slid his own deck out of his battered messenger bag and was passing the cards between his hands.

"What is it you're afraid people might find out that would give them the wrong impression?" Moira asked.

"Everyone's got those sorts of things. Secrets."

Moira grinned at him. "I've never kept a secret in my life."

Rhys broke the deck into pieces and spun the cards between his fingers with the deftness of a stage illusionist.

"Well maybe someday I'll introduce you to my secrets," he said. His eyes were downcast, modest as an icon of Mary, but there was a devilish smile on his lips. He was flirting with her, most definitely.

"Where did you learn to shuffle like that?" she asked.

"An ex."

"A boy ex or a girl ex?"

Now Rhys looked at her, pure terror in his eyes. "Does it matter?"

Moira shrugged one shoulder, calculatedly casual. She hadn't meant to frighten him. Typically, she wouldn't care about the answer at all, but she had a growing vested interest in Rhys being attracted to women.

"Not particularly. Just making friendly conversation."

Rhys nodded a few times, as though to calm himself.

"My college boyfriend. Bit of a showboat." His eyes flicked up to meet hers for a split second. "I like girls too, though."

"That one of your secrets?" she said, keeping things playful to cover up the wave of relief that washed over her.

"Not a secret if I tell you, is it?" Rhys tossed the cards from one hand to another, then flipped over the Two of Swords with a flourish. "I might self-censor in certain company, but it looks like you can't make up your mind. So, what is it? Two job offers on the table? Couple of handsome strangers fighting for your heart?"

Moira rolled her shoulders and leaned back onto her hands, tipping her throat up towards the sky. She bathed in the moon for a moment, then said, "I guess... I don't really know what's next for me. If I should move back home or not."

"Where's home?"

"Georgia. A little hobby farm. Just my parents, six chickens, some wild cats, and a goat. Momma keeps talking about getting one of those miniature ponies, the ones with sour temperaments. I think it'd be a laugh."

Rhys set his deck down beside her own. "You love that place, huh?"

"So much. The summer thunderstorms, the fall colors, the honey harvest... My parents have always let me know I could come back home after graduation. I just don't know if I want to. I like New England fine, but it's cold in winter and the people are brusque, and to be honest they're just as racist as they are down South. At least if I went home, I would be surrounded by people who love me... But I've never been one for going backwards."

"What's your major?"

"Fashion. I thought I wanted to be a designer. But it turns out most fashion students are nepo babies with no taste. I couldn't imagine spending my entire career around them. What about you?"

"I just graduated. Double major in classics and history. I want to be a librarian. Do you have a job in mind?"

Moira thought about this for a moment, weighing how honest she wanted to be with him. But it wasn't fair to needle him for wearing a mask when she wasn't willing to take hers off.

"Helping people," she said finally. "Giving them good counsel and a safe place to rest while they figure out what it is they ought to do about their problems. Whether that's through fortune telling or rootwork or positive psychology, I don't much mind."

"What about money?" he asked, curious.

"Oh, money seems to find me when I need it. I like taking odd jobs anyway. Doesn't tie me down."

Rhys nodded at her cards. "Can I touch them?"

"Knock yourself out," Moira said, pleased that he had been polite enough to ask. Some tarot readers were superstitious

about anyone touching their deck, so asking for permission
was always courteous.

Rhys ran his fingers along the edge of Moira's deck,
feeling the slight bow in the cards that had come from her
shuffling them the same direction for so many years. Moira
shuddered slightly, as though it was her spine he was trailing
his fingers along.

"So if school isn't your thing, what's keeping you up
here?" he asked.

A bead of mead ran down Moira's wrist as she tipped the
bottle back, and she lapped it up with a swipe of her tongue.

"There's a lot to love here, too," she said.

"In my experience, places are never the way you remember
them," Rhys said quietly, his expression darkening. "Even if
you find it the way you left it. You're the thing that changes."

Moira made a little humming sound in the back of her
throat. "Wise words. For that I'll give you another free
reading. One card only, an exclusive deal."

Moira cut her deck, then produced The Chariot.

Moira's deck was different from Rhys': where his illustrations were muted and pulled directly from classical Western
metaphysics, hers were vibrant, with whorls of color swirling
together to produce impressionistic scenes. The familiar
symbols most readers would expect, the scales and chalices
and crowns, were entirely absent. In Moira's deck, the
Chariot was a long luxurious car barreling through a rainy
night, with headlights blazing and a white dove fluttering
overhead.

"Oh, you're one of those types," she murmured. "Chariot
folks are driven as hell, natural born leaders, determined to
succeed and look good doing it. They hate being broke, too.
Most of all they *want*. Chariot people are made up of desires,

and they've got the power of will to bring those desires into fruition. So. What's a man want so bad he's willing to spend his solstice summoning spirits in the middle of a field?"

Rhys beamed, reckless and golden. "The world, to start."

Moira snorted and shook her head.

"You mean to tell me," Rhys persisted, "that if you could somehow get in contact with ancient, powerful beings with knowledge of psychics, astrology, the passage of time, the measure of a man's soul... You wouldn't take advantage of that? You wouldn't want to know?"

Moira couldn't keep the fondness out of her smile. "You've got a bit of a poetic streak in there too, don't you?" Then her face fell a bit. "Nothing's worth your soul, Rhys. Or didn't you ever hear that song about the devil and a fiddle?"

"This isn't the devil. At least not in the way you're imagining. These things, these spirits, they're all over the spectrum. Some are benevolent, or tricksters, or wise, or just plain confused. And yes, some may be malicious, some may be looking to get more than they're willing to give, but they're easy enough to identify. It's like that bit in Corinthians about the discernment of spirits; it's a skill to be honed, if you have it." Rhys passed his hands over his face, like his world was spinning. "Sorry, I'm getting carried away... Are you Catholic?"

"I'm Southern."

"What's that mean?"

"Where I'm from, even the Catholics are Baptist."

"Alright, well I don't really consider myself super religious or anything but... We're talking about the forces that laid the foundation of the earth, the energies that keep the whole thing going; beings with direct access to God, Source, the Universe, whatever it ends up being in the end."

Moira watched him intently, the Chariot card warm as a sun-bathed stone under her fingers. He was finally letting his guard down, and Moira liked that a lot.

"Magic is a technology," he continued, voice a little softer but no less intense. "It's neither good nor bad, just a neutral skill to be used by a competent practitioner. And the way I see it, God didn't ban learning how to read or how to make bricks, so why this?"

Moira gently moved the mead bottle out of the way, leaned forward to take his face in her hands, and stopped centimeters short of a kiss.

"You don't mind, do you?" she asked, poised on the precipice of rejection but still brave enough to jump.

Rhys marveled at her, his dark eyes shaded by short, full lashes.

"I've been waiting for you to kiss me since I got into this truck," he said.

So Moira kissed him, drinking him in and taking her time.

She lingered close after she pulled away, and he reached up to brush his knuckle under her chin. When he spoke, his voice was quiet.

"Do you really want to know what I wanted so badly that I started teaching myself magic?"

"Yes," she whispered, taking in the electricity of this moment, its fragility and promise.

"I wanted to go to Williams. I wanted it so bad I couldn't think of anything else. I had a B average and working-class parents and no professional connections. I was willing to do anything."

Rhys's eyes were bright as polished tourmaline. Black tourmaline kept evil away, Moira remembered absently, and she wondered if that had anything to do with how safe she felt around him.

"It's just a school though, isn't it?" Moira said gently. "At the end of the day."

"It didn't feel that way then. It felt like my only ticket out of obscurity; the fast track to status and influence and people who mattered. I was dumb."

"So your spells didn't work?"

"Oh, they worked alright. And I got the worst thing possible. Exactly what I wanted, with nowhere to go and everything to prove. I spent four years feeling like I had no right to be there, like I cheated. The way I see it, real magic always asks a sacrifice of us, and that was what I gave up to get into Williams: my joy."

She ran her hand up his arm, coming to rest with her palm pressed against his heart. Rhys pressed a courteous kiss to the corner of her mouth to see if her lips would part for him, and smirked when they did.

Then suddenly, he pulled away. "Shit. The alignment: what time is it?"

Moira glanced at her watch. "Oh honey, you don't want to know."

Rhys stood and stepped gingerly back from her cards, suddenly looking very self-conscious. "I'm so sorry, I didn't mean to keep you from your ritual–"

"Ritual?" Moira asked, arching an eyebrow. "I didn't come out to do any kind of ritual; I just came out here to harvest some dirt. Crossroad dirt's good for all sorts of things."

Rhys blinked dumbly as she rose to press her palms against her lower back and stretch, her belly almost touching his as she surveyed the stars.

"That's it?" he asked with a laugh. "You were going to kick me out of a crossroads for some dirt?"

"There's a certain procedure to the whole thing that I don't like to be disturbed. And magic doesn't have to be complicated to be strong. Give me a little crossroads dirt, some red thread, and a couple of nails and I can make your life quite unpleasant. It's too bad you didn't get to do your ritual, though. Sorry about that one."

"Oh," Rhys said, looking down at his abandoned circle in the dirt. "It's alright. It wasn't life or death."

"What were you going to ask for once you got the critter into the circle? Let me guess: fabulous wealth? No, the destruction of your enemies!"

Rhys cleared his throat. "Um. I was just going to ask for a name."

"Not going to tell me, hmm?" Moira chuckled. "Was it the name of your true love, maybe?"

"Still," Rhys said quickly. "I'm sorry, uh, about your dirt."

"I'll let you make it up to me."

"Oh?"

"You can take me out." Moira kissed his jaw once, feather-light and coy. Then she was gone, crouched down in the truck bed, sliding her tarot cards back into their embroidered bag. "One time only exclusive offer."

Rhys hopped out of the truck and watched her pack up with his hands stuffed into his back pockets. She passed parcels and bottles back into their boxes, trying to hide her twitterpated smile in the dark.

"I can make it worth your time," Rhys said, a little bolder now, a little more sure.

Moira looked up and grinned at him. "I expect nothing less than a magical evening."

The Chariot

CHAPTER SEVEN

RHYS

"I cannot believe you are letting the whole Society traipse through our house," Moira muttered. She was watering a bouquet of spray roses and chrysanthemums displayed in a mason jar on the kitchen counter while Rhys set the kettle to boiling.

"It's not the whole Society, Moira," he sighed. Moira had a bad habit of waiting right up until the last minute to indicate her disapproval about anything, like the time she had confessed that she didn't actually like opera while they were in the car on the way to the theatre. Or like now, when she was kicking off a spat about the Society when the brothers who had so graciously agreed to help were no more than ten minutes away.

"Might as well be," she muttered.

"My membership in the Society is important to me," Rhys said, with the weary mildness of someone who was well-accustomed to walking the same lines of argument over and over. "Half of what I know, I learned from them.

I trust their expertise. Besides, we're out of options. I can't sleep in this house, I can't get any work done, I can't even use the study anymore… It's the best shot we have."

Moira's brow knitted together as she touched the rotting stems of her flowers. Rhys often surprised her with bundles of in-season blossoms tied with creamy ribbons. These gifts usually lasted for some time, but this bouquet had taken on an ashen pallor mere hours after being brought into the house. More spirit meddling, Rhys supposed. Or maybe he had merely picked the wrong flowers. When in doubt, he tended to fall back on blaming himself.

"That doesn't mean I want them setting up shop in my living room," she said.

Rhys poured steaming water over the coffee grounds in the French press.

"I don't know what else you want me to do, Moira. We need help. And it isn't the whole Society; it's just David and some of the younger guys. You said you were on board with the plan last night."

Moira swept a few dead leaves off the counter and into the trash can. "I know what I said," she grumbled.

"Would you light the candles, please?"

Rhys passed her the box of matchsticks, and she began to fill their kitchen with the aroma of wick-smoke and lemon verbena wax. Rhys had been fussing around the house all morning, sweeping out the front hall and stuffing stray coats and discarded shoes into the closet. He was somewhere between being humiliated for having to ask for help from the Society and being thrilled that they had so quickly offered to assist in any way they could. He was still a young initiate, and he still had a lot to prove.

He had spent an hour talking Moira through the idea,

listening to her fears and hesitations, and offering possible alternative solutions. She had come fully on board, at least at the time. Now, she was intent on making her cold feet both their problems.

The doorbell chimed.

"I'll get it," Rhys said, already halfway down the hallway.

"We'll both get it," Moira replied.

Rhys took a breath and reminded himself to smile as he opened the door.

Three members of the Society stood on the front porch, scrolling through emails on their iPhones or straightening their cuffs in the glass of the door. Many of the members of the Society were older and had children and mortgages, but these men were closer to Rhys's age and a spent a lot of their time at three-mimosa brunches gossiping about the older set.

One of them, a man in his late twenties with deliberately tousled bronze hair, smiled down at Moira like he was trying to sell her something. Rhys knew David Aristarkhov well enough to know that this was his approximation of friendliness. But sometimes, as far as David was concerned, his overtures at niceness were worse than his natural inclination towards being disagreeable. Especially where Moira was concerned.

"Mrs McGowan," David said. "It's a pleasure to see you again."

"McGowan is my husband's name," Moira replied icily. "I'm a Delacroix. But yes David, nice to see you too."

"Come in," Rhys said, too quickly.

Moira had met the men gathered on his doorstep a few times before, at Christmas parties or meet-the-missus dinners, and she had interacted with David the most, but that hadn't endeared them to each other. Maybe it would always feel chilly when David and Moira were in the same room. Rhys hoped not.

David put a hand on Rhys's shoulder and kissed the air next to his cheek. A little bit of European posturing he had picked up while summering in Capri.

"You look like you haven't slept in a week," he said. A typical greeting for David.

"Coffee?" Rhys asked, grasping for some sense of normalcy. David and Moira were two forces of nature most safely kept separate, and Rhys felt like a little boat adrift on a churning sea while storm clouds gathered overhead.

"Always," David said.

Moira drifted into the kitchen as the men congregated around her stove, her lips pressed into a thin line. David leaned against the marble-topped kitchen island and prattled away while Rhys brewed the coffee. As always, David was impeccably dressed, in a pinstriped shirt of lightest blue and chinos that fit so well they had to be tailored.

"I was up until two last night trying to get hold of this woman's dead husband," David was saying. "We must have sat at her kitchen table for an hour with her squeezing my hands hard enough to crush bone. Then, when he finally showed up, she spent another hour nagging him about the state he left their finances in. With a wife like that no wonder his heart gave out at forty-nine."

Chuckles rippled through the kitchen and David laughed at his own joke, white teeth flashing in his blitheness. Moira pushed herself up onto the counter and sat as far out of the way as possible. Rhys cast a glance at her, calculating a way to draw her into conversation, but she had her arms strapped over her chest, a clear indication that she was in no mood to chat.

"You're still seeing clients, then?" Rhys asked David. Strictly speaking, these men were his friends, but they were also his competition for recognition and advancement in the Society. Rhys weighed his words carefully around them. "I figured you wouldn't have time after becoming a prosecutor."

"I try to find the time. There's always money in mediumship." David arched his neck to look over Rhys's shoulder at Moira. "I appreciate your referrals, by the way. Your clients speak very highly of you. Apparently, you're a miracle worker."

"I do what I can," Moira said, the words rehearsed in her mouth. She had decided upon their first meeting that she did not like David, and despite David's occasional attempts at sweetness, Moira's first impressions were hard for anyone to recover from. "Most of the time I end up helping the client heal themselves. It's a privilege."

"Oh, I'm sure. You should get into spirit work, though. Summoning, channeling, that sort of thing. It can really take your magical practice to the next level, and those are the skills in the highest demand."

"Thanks, David," Moira said flatly.

Rhys took a deep breath in through his nose and tried to remain calm. Sometimes, David "making an effort" was worse than David making no effort at all.

"Are you a psychic too?" Nathan, one of the other members of the Society, asked. He had been inducted mere months ago, and Rhys hadn't known much about him other than his having gotten $250,000 in venture capital funding for his startup with the help of seven lesser spirits. Rhys could be downright aggressive with new blood, as competitive as he was, but Nathan had quickly proven himself to be a people-pleaser who was into occultism more as a social club than anything else. Rhys had never met anyone who was so easy to get along with, and they had become fast friends.

"Not in so many words," Moira said, thawing slightly. Good, that was good. Maybe Rhys could handle David and direct the conversation so Moira spent most of her time with Nathan, whom she seemed to like better. He wanted her to feel as comfortable as possible. This was her house, after all, no matter how inhospitable it had become. "I offer a wide range of tailored services depending on the clients' needs."

"Moira's practice is incredibly multifaceted," Rhys offered. He never passed up an opportunity to boast about her achievements. "She reads tarot, she calculates natal charts, she even writes her own spells."

"Oh, that's very modern," David said, and there it was, that thread of cattiness in his voice. The same thread that had once felt like it would strangle Rhys if he didn't cut the cord himself.

"Her practice is well-adapted to the 21st century," Rhys said firmly. "I wish I could say the same for the Society."

"I think that's great! It sounds like you've got a fan following going already," Nathan said. Softly, he teased her, like he was encouraging her to come outside and play ball with him. "We'd better watch out, or you might start your own secret society."

Moira finally smiled. Rhys smiled in return as he watched her unfurl slowly, like a flower seeking the sun.

"So long as I don't end up a penniless madman like Aleister Crowley, I think I'll be fine," she said, throwing in a reference to one of the last century's greatest occultists, just to show that she had done the reading. Rhys was proud of her. She had caught the ball Nathan had tossed to her and thrown it back expertly.

Moira, Nathan, and Rhys shared a laugh.

"You should be so lucky," David said smoothly. It was hard to say if he was trying to shoot her down, or if he was trying to edge his way back into the conversation, as uncomfortable as he was when he wasn't in the spotlight. "Crowley was a visionary. They don't call him the father of modern occultism for nothing."

The blossom in Moira's ribcage folded back in on itself, and her giggles dried up.

"Well," Rhys said, shooting daggers at David. Rhys could have killed him. He really could have. "He did do an awful lot of heroin."

Cameron Casillas, an adjunct professor at a nearby divinity school, put down his coffee with a gentle clink. Cameron was quiet and often humorless, but he was an excellent mediator.

"Bring us up to speed, Rhys. What exactly has been going on here? How can we help?"

Rhys took a deep breath as he continued to prepare coffee orders from memory. A dribble of cream and nothing else for David, black for Cameron, cream and two sugars for Nathan. He was good with details. With people, less so.

"Moira and I are being harassed in our own home. We haven't had any luck identifying what type of entity it might be or what it might want. David, I hoped you could help with that."

"Could it be a ghost?" David asked.

"No. That we could handle."

"Demons?" David suggested, his eyebrows shooting up as though he would enjoy such a dramatic turn.

"There's been some malevolent activity but nothing textbook," Moira put in.

"Very unusual," Cameron said, adjusting his glasses.

"It started up about a month ago–" Rhys began, but before he could finish his statement, the cabinets above his head began rattling vigorously.

David stood at attention, every inch of him alive. The rattling stopped as suddenly as it had started, and Nathan let out an impressed,

"Shit."

David shushed him with a few fingers held up in his direction. The psychic was listening intently with his head cocked.

The rattling started up again, this time in a cabinet on the opposite side of the room, and Rhys jolted at the sudden sound. David breezed past him and approached the wall nearest the possessed cabinet. David closed his eyes and pressed his palm flush against the wall. The cabinet banged furiously, hinges creaking with the strain, and then all was silent once again.

David's eyes snapped open.

"Show me the rest of the house."

With a new urgency, the men drifted out of the kitchen with David in the lead. He dawdled in the front hall, examining family pictures and dusty corners while tapping the labradorite ring he was wearing against his coffee cup. Rhys had never seen him without the ring, and he knew that labradorite imparted strength and boosted psychic ability in the wearer. Unlike other members of the Society, who enforced a sharp delineation between their magical practices and personal presentation, David liked to drop little hints for those who knew what they were looking for. It was probably why Rhys had been drawn to David in the first place, back in college when David had introduced him to the Society.

Back when Rhys and David had gotten tangled up in each other fast before burning through all of each other's goodwill. Despite how volatile magician-on-magician relationships tended to be, Rhys had always liked magical people.

"There's a definite heaviness to the house," David narrated. "A sense of presence." He ran a hand along the antique wallpaper and then the staircase banister. "But the energy is… I don't know, diffuse. Hard to characterize."

His fingers settled around the ornamental bulb at the end of the banister and found a thin chain haphazardly draped around it.

"Does this belong to anyone?" he asked, holding up Moira's infinity knot necklace.

Rhys took it from him quickly, as though David's touch might defile something sacred to Moira, and pressed it into Moira's hand. While David continued monologuing about the house's energetic matrix, Rhys said to his wife in a low voice, "You didn't actually lose this, did you? Something took it."

"I left it in my jewelry box one night and it was gone the next morning," she whispered, looking a little sick. "I didn't tell you because I didn't want to upset you. I don't know how—"

They teetered on the precipice of revelation, poised right on the edge of unraveling the truth together, but then David's voice shattered the moment.

"Anything electromagnetic?" David called as he jogged up the stairs.

"Flickering lights," Rhys said, pulling himself up the stairs after David. "Static on the doorknobs."

"Voices from other rooms?"

"Occasionally. Always indistinct."

This was familiar, this was comforting. Volleying magical theories back and forth with David, slotting the world into tidy categories. Order from chaos.

David paused on the landing to crane his neck down the hallway. "What room is that?"

"Moira's."

David shot Rhys a question with his eyes, and Moira intercepted it.

"My meditation room," she said. "We share the master bedroom, obviously."

"Obviously," David assured her, but it felt like placation. Rhys was reminded of why he and David didn't talk much out of Society meetings and group social events, at least not anymore. Maybe inviting David over had been a mistake, but it was too late to walk it back now. "Do you mind if I have a look inside?"

"Knock yourself out," Moira said.

The door swung open when David touched the handle lightly, and David staggered back as though he had been hit by a wave of overpowering perfume. He turned his face away from the room and blinked a few times.

"What's wrong?" Rhys asked, drawn to David's side despite himself. The instinct was an old one, carved into his bones: to clean up after David's whirlwind personality broke things, especially when the thing that got broken was David himself.

"Nothing's wrong," David said. He rotated his hands in a fluid motion around his face, as though clearing the air of smoke. "It's just that room."

"What's the matter with my room?" Moira demanded.

"Nothing," David repeated as he closed the door. "But you've stuffed it full of rose quartz. I've never seen so much in one place before. How do you work in there?

It must make the space so drowsy! Rose quartz in a baby's nursery, sure, but a room for magical workings? I would have chosen a different stone."

"Rose quartz isn't just for babies," Moira said, enunciating every word with damning clarity. She was definitely pissed. This was he and Moira's problem to solve, and it had left the ties that bound them brittle. He shouldn't have taken it at face value when she told him she was comfortable with the idea; he should have pressed more to be absolutely sure. "It draws unconditional love, heals trauma, mends relationships... It's just as powerful as that labradorite on your hand, but more stable."

David smiled at her as he slipped into the bedroom she shared with her husband. "To each their own."

The master bedroom was a haphazard collection of curtains and pillows in moody teals and sea foam greens that somehow, when arrayed together, made sense. A well-worn sage armchair by the windowsill still had one of Rhys's hermetic texts sitting open on it, and the room smelled faintly of the palo santo water Moira spritzed on their sheets.

David moved through the room briskly, uninterested in what he found, until his eye caught a small photo in a silver frame on the bedside table. He grinned and picked it up fondly.

"Oh, God."

"What is it?" Rhys asked as he kicked a discarded pair of jeans under the bed.

"It's us at Bailey's, back in college. You remember; they had those four dollar well drinks on Thursday nights? I didn't think any photos existed."

Rhys' blood roared in his ears.

He pressed through the other men to snag the picture out of David's hand.

"No, that's not right, this is a picture of Moira and I on our honeymoon…" His voice trailed off as his eyes beheld an over-exposed snapshot of him and David in a crowded nightclub, David's arm around his neck, Rhys's eyes squeezed shut with tipsy glee. Rhys remembered this night, if barely. He had spent an hour picking out an all-black outfit and smudging on eyeliner just to spend most of the night babysitting David, who had pre-gamed too hard as usual.

Moira took the photo from Rhys. He was freshly nineteen in the photo, sweaty-faced and vodka-flushed. The picture had been taken years before she had met him, but that didn't numb the strange sickness that wormed its way into his stomach.

"You said you hated going dancing," she said, pursing her lips tightly. "You never go with me."

"I do hate it," Rhys implored. He wanted to gather her into his arms, but everyone in the room was staring at him, and it was suddenly difficult to breathe. "Nightclubs give me anxiety."

Moira tossed the photograph down on the bed, her eyes fixed on the ground.

David seemed to notice then that he may have disrupted some of Rhys's matrimonial bliss, and to his credit, he looked a bit embarrassed about it.

"I was big into the club scene at the time; he only went to make me happy," David said to Moira. "It was like pulling teeth every time, let me tell you. And I wasn't exactly the cheapest date. Liquor and I don't mix anymore, for good reason."

It was perhaps the most vulnerable thing David had ever said to Moira, but she refused to meet his eyes. Ultimately, it was miscalculated, as Rhys didn't think the thought of her husband putting himself so far out of his comfort zone to make David happy would make Moira feel any better.

"Love, I don't know how that picture got there, I swear,"

Rhys said quickly. "It should be in an old box of college keepsakes in storage."

Something about this protestation revived David's interest in the photo, and he took it up from the bed and began to turn it over in his hands.

"David?" Rhys questioned. There was very little softness the word.

David hardly looked up from his examination. "It's your house, Rhys. I didn't put this here."

"Well, neither did I."

"Let's keep going," Moira said, voice hoarse. "I want to get this over with."

"Moira—" Rhys attempted, but David was already speaking, in command of the room once again.

"Have either of you been having any strange dreams recently? Dreams of a violent or sexual nature, that sort of thing?"

"No, neither of us," Rhys said.

David's eyes were pinned to Moira.

"Ms Delacroix?"

"Everyone gets bad dreams," she said, more defensive than Rhys had ever seen her. Her eyes gleamed hard like river stones. "I've been stressed."

"Well, which is it then?" Rhys asked, morbidly curious. "Violent or sexual?"

For a moment, she looked like she might cry, but when she spoke, her voice was flat and toneless.

"I keep having dreams about hooking up with people. Strangers, mostly. In cars, or elevators. Sometimes here, in the bedroom."

Rhys felt a little queasy, and then he hardened all over, like a delicate moth dipped in protective steel.

"Alright then," he said quietly.

David took a half-step towards Rhys, but stopped and lingered where he stood well away from the warring couple. Nathan shifted from foot to foot, trying to avoid the tension in the air, and Cameron hadn't bothered to come into the room. He was leaning against the banister outside, watching the domestic dispute with an air of pastoral concern.

When David spoke, he sounded more like a social worker than a psychic. "Ms Delacroix, are dreams like this normal for you?"

"Not particularly," she said quietly.

David nodded once. "Let's continue through the house."

Moira stepped out of the room and disappeared without another word

Rhys turned into the hallway and stalked down the long Persian runner. Someone may have tried to reach out to touch his arm, or it may have been the tickle of a spiderweb. Either way, he brushed it off and started down the stairs.

As soon as Moira reached the ground floor and guided Cameron and Nathan towards the study, David caught up with Rhys on the stairs and lowered his voice. He was speaking for Rhys's benefit alone now, and his tone was stripped of its usual bravado.

"Have you been involved in any high-risk conjurations lately? Listen, we've all called up things we can't put down, if you need help–"

"Whatever this is, I didn't summon it," Rhys responded, dropping his voice. There was something familiar about this, a parody of the way they used to whisper inside jokes to each other during Society meetings, that made his stomach churn. "I'm sure."

"What about her?" David asked, nodding his head in Moira's direction.

"This isn't Moira's fault either," Rhys said icily.

"I'm not accusing her of anything, but we have to look at every possibility. I know you two have been on the rocks lately, and that you love her–"

"If it's all the same to you, you're the last person I want relationship advice from."

"–but love can blind, Rhys. I'm just asking you–"

"We're not doing this; Moira isn't at fault," Rhys huffed. "For God's sake, be civil."

David's green eyes narrowed but he didn't argue. He just breezed past Rhys and came to stand at Moira's side.

She was posted at the heavy door to the study, with a hard expression fixed on her face. Moira subjected her husband to the scrutiny of her gaze for a few moments, and then addressed the whole assembly.

"We locked the study up days ago. I can't make promises about the state of things inside."

"You just… closed the door and forgot about the room?" Nathan asked, smoothing his dark hair away from his brow.

"We'd just gotten so tired of dealing with it." Rhys sighed. He wanted to lay down and sleep for a long time.

David looked down at Moira with an arched eyebrow. "If you please, Ms Delacroix."

Moira braced her hands on the door and shoved it open.

"Sweet Jesus," she muttered.

The High priestess

CHAPTER EIGHT

MOIRA

Pages torn from books – some commonplace, some priceless – littered the ground like flower petals at a wedding. Paintings hung askew, vases had been toppled, and watery dark spots bloomed across the wallpaper. Most disconcertingly, the Edwardian crystal chandelier, an estate-sale find that Rhys was painfully proud of, pulsed irregularly with eerie light. This could have perhaps been attributed to faulty wiring, except for the fact that the chandelier was pre-electrical in design and had never been hooked up to any grid.

David stepped into the center of the room, unclasped his cufflinks, and rolled up his sleeves. The tattoo inside his right forearm of the monas hieroglyphica caught the light as he raised his arms and spread his fingers.

"I want everyone in a circle," he said.

Moira chose to position herself between Nathan and Cameron instead of next to Rhys. She wasn't feeling very close to her husband at the moment, especially not after the

74

strange appearance of that photo in their bedroom and the humiliation of admitting to her dreams, and she certainly wasn't going to stand next to David. That meant she and Rhys ended up standing directly across from each other in the circle, trying not to catch each other's eyes.

"I need everyone to be quiet and focus," David said. "Close your eyes if that's your thing, I don't really care, but I want everyone psychically present. I will ask you to hold hands, and it's imperative that you do not break that connection for the duration of the ceremony. If we don't have a circle to draw the spirit into, I can't safely question, bind, or banish it."

"What is this, a seance?" Moira said. Cameron reached out for her hand, but she pulled away. She was starting to feel a little panicky. She should have never agreed to this. "I don't want any kind of seance happening in this house. Go do that somewhere else."

"A seance is generally used to communicate with the dead," David said mildly, letting his eyes slide shut. "And if it's trafficking with the dead you're worried about, don't be. Whatever this thing is, it's very much alive. I'm going to reach out to it."

"What are you gonna do, try and read its mind?"

David cracked open an eye. "Mind reading is a parlor trick. Channeling is an art. Are you going to cooperate or not?"

The temperature in the room slid downwards, and Moira felt goosebumps prickle on her arms.

"David, she just told you she doesn't feel good about this," Rhys said, and even though he couldn't look at his wife, she was grateful that he spoke up. Even when they were most at odds, they refused to let anyone but each other deal the damage. "Can't she step outside?"

"I need everyone present and accounted for," David said. "I'm testing a theory. Nathan, get the drapes."

The venture capitalist made the rounds, tugging every curtain in the room closed, then returned to his spot in the circle.

"I've been doing this for fifteen years," David went on. "I'm asking you all to trust me."

Anger uncoiled in Moira's chest, as sharp-fanged as a snake.

"Okay, indigo child," she sniped. "Show us those hundred-dollar-an-hour skills."

David's eyes widened slightly as he looked at Moira, really looked at her, like he was finally seeing her for exactly what she was. A powerful magical practitioner in her own right, and a threat to his ironclad control over the room.

"I'm sorry, do you have a problem with the way I do consultancy?" he said, his tone sliding from professional to petulant. She was getting to him. Moira smiled right back, as sweet as poisoned pie. There was something deeply satisfying about making David Aristarkhov sweat.

"You can hardly call it consultancy if it isn't accessible to the average person."

David dropped his hands to his sides. "I can't work like this."

"This is my house," Moira snapped.

The chandelier had grown more erratic, and it cast an eerie glow on their faces in the darkened room.

"Your bad attitude is going to put us in danger," David replied, and now she knew she was winning, because he sounded more like a teenager throwing a tantrum than anything else.

"David, that's enough," Rhys said. "Watch how you talk to my wife, or I'm calling this whole thing off."

"Rhys–" David protested.

"Switch places with Moira," Rhys said, leaving no room for argument.

David and Moira crossed the circle past each other, the vehemence between them enough to make the air crackle with static electricity. Rhys snagged his wife's hand and held it tightly.

Once David was repositioned, he held out his hands, closed his eyes, and said, "Let's begin."

All Moira could hear was the sound of her furious heartbeat and the slowing breathing of the men around her. She shut her eyes tighter, ignoring the squeeze of Rhys's fingers. Her anger had been released, and she didn't want his touch right now or his rising to her defense. She wanted to lay into David and take him down a few pegs all by herself.

For a long moment, there was total silence. The stillness of a morgue.

Then, just as Moira was starting to itch from standing still so long, a draft crossed her skin. Stray hairs that had come loose from her bun stirred around her face, and she felt a shiver travel up Rhys's arm.

"We've come seeking contact with the spirit of this house," David began, in a smooth, authoritative tenor that Moira suspected he also used in the courtroom. "If you are with us, give us a sign."

Another few minutes of quiet crawled by. Moira felt certain that the room was getting colder, but she didn't know how that was possible, as the early fall weather had been temperate thus far.

"Give us a sign," David repeated. "Any sign. We'll wait."

They did wait, for another minute or more, before a soft rattling sounded from the curio cabinet. The delicate collectibles clattered against each other.

"Don't be coy," David said, a smile in his voice.

The rattling jumped from the curio cabinet to the chandelier.

Thousands of pieces of cut glass began to swirl and clink against each other, until the entire study was filled with a dull crystalline roar. Moira trembled as the sound swelled up around her, but she held fast to the men at her side.

"You *are* powerful," David went on. "Speak with us, spirit. Do you love this house? Knock once for no and twice for yes."

Moira started as a pair of books fell off the shelf behind her, hitting the ground with two heavy, distinct *thuds*.

"Did you die here?"

Another *thud*, a little further away.

David breathed in through his nose and exhaled slowly, settling in. Moira got the impression that everything up until this point had been a warm-up.

"Were you summoned into this home by one of its occupants?" David asked, the question hanging in the air.

Rhys caught his wife's gaze for a fraction of a second before closing his eyes again.

This time, a dish of spare change on the desk was knocked over, and coins went bouncing and rolling across the floor.

Nathan looked a bit pale.

"Does that count as one or two?" he whispered to Moira. She shook her head, unsure how to answer.

David's eyes were roaming around the room, at random it seemed, but then they latched onto something.

Moira realized, with a creeping sense of dread, that he was tracking a target she couldn't see.

"David," she said, her voice high and thin.

He kept his eyes fixed on whatever was moving slowly past Nathan and nearer to Moira. When David's eyes passed over her head, Moira felt something papery-soft brush across the back of her arms.

"Oh my God," she gasped. "Something touched me! Rhys something–"

"Speak plainly," David interrupted, his eyes moving from Moira to the air behind Rhys's head. "Or I will make you."

Rhys stiffened beside her as he took a shaky breath. "David–"

"Rhys, keep it together," David replied.

"I can feel it breathing," Rhys said, teeth gritted. "On the back of my neck."

"I'm working on it."

Rhys shuddered and tilted his face to the ceiling, squeezing his eyes shut.

"God – it's–"

"Touching your shoulder, I know." David's voice took on an even more authoritarian edge. "Why are you hiding behind them, hmm? Come out here and let me look at you. That's what you want, isn't it, to be seen? Noticed? Come into the circle."

Moira's heart missed a beat as a thick miasma of sadness lurched through her body, and Rhys swayed beside her as though he were going to lose consciousness. She was left with pins and needles in her fingers and the awful sensation that she had been passed through as easily as any door.

David pulled the hands of the two men he was standing between together, joined them, and slipped into the circle without breaking it. The ring of bodies tightened, bringing them all closer.

"The high priest told you not to do that," Cameron sighed. Moira got the impression that David was known for breaking rules on the fly.

"The high priest isn't here," David said. "Steer the course."

David approached whatever awaited him in the center of the circle with slow, deliberate steps. The chandelier above his head hummed dangerously, pulsing with a phantom glow.

Despite the dim light, Moira could make out a shadow where one ought not to be, hovering just a few feet away from David. Her eyes stung, and there was a headache building at the base of her skull, but she could see it plain as day.

"Do you see that?" Moira whispered to Rhys.

Her husband shook his head, then turned to David, nearly burning a hole into David's skull with his eyes.

"This is reckless," Rhys said, mouth set into an unforgiving line. David didn't acknowledge him. He was captivated by the black mass hovering a few feet away. It was difficult to tell in the low lighting, but Moira thought that, somehow, it was taking on a humanoid shape.

"Come on," David urged the manifestation, "you don't need to be shy. Let me see you."

"We need to take the right precautions," Rhys said, louder this time. "People have died from going into a circle unprepared."

David was reaching out with splayed fingers towards the creature, shifting further and further into smokey perceptibility.

"Come here. Speak through me; let me advocate for you. Tell us what you want."

Moira's scalp was tingling, the hair on her arms standing upright.

David was inches away from it now, every muscle in his body coiled tight with anticipation. David, who Moira had so often seen looking bored by the world and its offerings, David, who had been working as a psychic consultant since he was a teen and had seen everything in the book. David, who could perhaps be excited by nothing but the strangest and most dangerous of supernatural phenomena.

His face was riveted. He had no intention of stopping.

"This Society has rules for a reason," Rhys said. "You have to follow them."

Something about this pricked at David, and he broke his attention away from the spirit just long enough to shoot Rhys a dirty look.

"With all due respect Rhys, that attitude is exactly why we broke up."

Moira's heart fell into her stomach at the same moment the black mass shuddered forward to wrap a terribly dark, terribly real tendril of a hand around David's wrist.

"Fuck you," her husband said, almost too quiet for Moira to hear, and tore his hands free from the circle. Moira was aware that their circle was the only thing stabilizing the manifestation, but even that knowledge couldn't have prepared her for the chaos that followed.

A cold wind burst through the windows. The shadow figure fluctuated wildly, fizzling and swelling as it rushed up David's arm to claw at his face. David staggered back a few paces and gasped for help, but by the time Cameron rushed into the circle to assist him, the psychic had been almost entirely consumed by the shadows.

"The lights!" Moira yelled. Nathan rushed to tear open the curtains as she felt along the wall for the switch.

Moira slammed on the lights and spun around to find David sprawled on the study floor, white as a sheet. His forearms were scraped up as though he had skinned himself after taking a bad fall. A thin trickle of blood ran from his nicked jaw.

He brought a hand up to his neck and pulled it away to examine the tacky smear of red on his fingers, then glowered at Rhys. As though, somehow, this was entirely Rhys' fault.

"I had everything under control," David said.

Rhys banged open his desk drawer, and stiffly tossed a box of Band-Aids at David's feet.

"I specifically asked you to just–" Rhys took a deep breath, as though reminding himself to breathe might be the only thing preventing him from losing composure entirely. "– look around."

"You asked for my help, and now you're mad I gave it to you. Is this how you thank someone for spending their Saturday doing charity work?" David rifled through the box and slapped a Band-Aid on his neck, then rolled down his sleeves to cover up the lesions. He pulled himself to his feet, straightened his collar with a huff, and then he was himself again. "I'll remember that in the future."

"Don't be dramatic," Rhys said. He shot a glance to Moira, meeting her eyes with a precarious sort of uncertainty. He seemed to be searching for something inside her, some reprieve or relief that he couldn't quite find. "You haven't helped us at all, David."

"Haven't I?" David asked. "Why don't we confirm a suspicion, then?"

He snagged the battered tarot box from Rhys's desk and slid the gold-foiled cards into his hands. He shuffled them with a modified sybil cut, one of Rhys's standbys when he was trying to make new friends at parties.

He fanned the cards through his hands, presenting an even sliver of each card back, and proffered them to Moira, who was still trying to catch her breath over by the light switch.

"Ms Delacroix?" he said.

"Me?" Moira asked. Her head was swimming from what she had just witnessed. As a healer she had seen people break down, burst into tears, or recount their traumas in excruciating detail. As a witch she had delved deep into the collective unconscious through dreams, trance meditation, and herbal concoctions. She had broken curses that were ruining people's lives and cast spells that changed her own waking reality. But she had never seen anything like this.

"Yes, you," David said, the picture of poise.

"You don't have to listen to him," Rhys said, holding his palm up in a soothing gesture. As though she was a wild doe that might bolt. "We've all had a long day. This was obviously a terrible idea, and for that I apologize. I think we should call it here."

"He's right, you don't have to listen," David said with a shrug. "And you don't have to ever find out what's attacking you either. It's your funeral."

Moira's mother had always said her curiosity would kill her someday. Neither fear nor love stood a chance to stop Moira when she got an inkling into her mind about something, when that burning desire to *know* flared up inside her. It had exhausted her mother when she was a girl, Moira's incessant questions, her constant pushing of boundaries, but her grandmother had always said it was one of her greatest assets. When offered a choice between blissful ignorance and even the most painful of truths, Moira would always choose to know.

"Please," David said, when she still hadn't taken a step forward. There was something oddly pleading in his voice, as though this had at some point stopped being a game and become something more dire, and that was enough to break her trance.

She drifted across the study and stood before the pair of men, David on her left, Rhys on her right. When she spoke, her voice was hardly more than a whisper.

"What in the hell is going on here?"

"Rhys was right," David said, and to his credit, he spoke gently. The rest of the world fell away as he pinned her in place with those eyes, green as sea glass. She could see how someone could lose themselves in those eyes, especially if they didn't know him very well. "This isn't a haunting. And it's nothing either of you summoned in a ritual. I just need your help with some further clarification."

Moira turned to her husband. Rhys's lips were parted, his eyes shining with intensity, as he looked from Moira to David and then back again. The married couple held each other's gaze for a long time, sharing the weight of the moment, and then Rhys gave the tiniest of nods.

Moira reached out and chose a card.

The design stood out starkly, gold gilt on black: three swords plunging into a heart while church bells tolled in the background. The Three of Swords, the card of heartbreak and betrayal – of love irrevocably lost.

Moira cried out as though she had been pierced.

Rhys reached out for Moira, but David stepped between them before they could touch, removing the card from Moira's fingers and tossing it down on the desk. Then he turned from the couple and started to pull on his coat.

"David, explain," Rhys said tightly. He couldn't look at his ex, or at his wife. He just kept staring at the card on the table. "Now."

"It's a tulpa," David sighed, as though it were as clear as the blue of the sky. "A thoughtform. About ten times more powerful than the ones we made in college, but a thoughtform all the same."

Moira was slipping in slow-motion like Alice down the rabbit hole. Possible interpretations of the card flickered through her mind: deceit, divorce, infidelity, and grief, unfolding in ever-increasing nightmares.

"I've never heard of anyone in the real world successfully creating one," Moira spat. "That's Reddit forum armchair magician psychobabble. I don't even know how they're supposed to operate. So how could I have possibly made one?'

"A tulpa is a being created on the astral plane by the will of a magician," Rhys said, definitions coming to him easily even when articulating his emotions did not. He pressed his fingertips against the wood of his desk until they went white. "Whether through ritual or visualization, repetition and intent keep them alive. The tulpa David and I made in college was just something we did on a dare, something to pass time. It was barely more than a shared hallucination. But some tulpas become strong enough to act on their own and affect the material world." He finally turned to David, a storm cloud passing over his face. "Tell me you aren't suggesting what I think you are."

"The evidence is quite unanimous," David said. "I'll bet you every time something has gone wrong in this house it's been right after you two had a tiff. Tell me I'm wrong."

Moira radiated contempt. She had never been the one to start fights on the playground, but the urge to knock David to the ground like the school bully he was and rub his face into the carpet until his moisturized cheeks were burned was overwhelming.

"I would *never* do anything to hurt Rhys," she said through gritted teeth. She could barely get the words out.

"Not on purpose, sure," David went on. She couldn't tell if he was a little scared of her, or a little impressed, or both. "But I have you three for three with the cupboards, the photo, and the chandelier. Every one of those things happened when you were upset. That thing was acting out your impulses."

"This is insane," Rhys said. "I'm going to give you one chance to walk this back before–"

"Before what? I touched it, Rhys," David snapped. The glint of irritation that had flashed in his eyes when Rhys rebuked him for entering the circle was back. "I felt all that shame and rage. It's a tulpa. Case closed."

"Why would my *wife* go through all that trouble to create something that's been tormenting us for a month?" Rhys demanded, his pitch on the edge of a raised voice. Moira expected David to match his volume, but he kept quiet and calm.

"I'm not saying she did it intentionally. And I'm not saying she did it alone. Do you understand what I'm trying to tell you?"

"Get out, David. I want you gone."

David stood his ground, flickering another strange green glance to Moira before speaking again.

"The worst affected part of the house is the study, Rhys, *your* study. I know you well enough to know you've probably been barricading yourself in here to brood, and you've no doubt been feeding it your frustration the entire time. I think you two have some serious problems that are spilling into the astral plane." He spread his fingers, like Pilate absolving himself of Christ's spilled blood. "That's just my opinion, but I'll remind you that you asked for it."

In the resulting silence, you could have heard a pin drop. Rhys glowered at his shoes and Moira scowled up at David and David paused politely for a few moments, his face serene, until he glanced at his watch.

"You're an asshole, do you know that?" Moira said.

The psychic gave a small shrug.

"I wasn't trying to embarrass either of you. But the truth isn't always nice, Ms Delacroix, and it's certainly not often pretty. I'm not going to apologize for that."

In that moment she hated him so powerfully her previous distaste felt like the inside of a greeting card.

"Get out of my house," Rhys said, his voice all the more vehement for its quietness.

"Fine," David said crisply. Some unspoken electricity crackled between then, an old bitterness Moira didn't understand and didn't care to. "I'm not a marriage counselor. Sort this out yourselves."

He moved to the other men, muttering something as they trailed behind him on their way out the door. Nathan looked tempted to linger, but Rhys shook his head and waved him on.

David paused on the threshold, his voice as light and casual as it had been when he arrived.

"I'll see you at the Society meeting, Rhys."

When the door at last swung closed behind him, it sounded like a tomb being shut.

The Chariot

CHAPTER NINE

RHYS

Moira rounded on Rhys the moment she heard the front door close. Rhys knew very well that his wife was a difficult person to anger, but once she tipped over the edge into rage, there was no talking her down until the fire had burned through her system.

"I can't believe you let him humiliate me like that!"

Rhys was unsteady on his feet, lightheaded from the fiasco of the last hour. Somehow, that had gone worse than he could have possibly imagined. A muscle in his palm was twitching and there was a sour, metallic tang in his mouth.

Fear, maybe. Or anger.

"*You* were humiliated?" he shot back, without thinking, without breathing. "What about me? Those are my colleagues, not yours. You don't have to face them every week."

Moira let out a bitter laugh. It ate at Rhys like rot in the support beams of a house.

"Sure, Rhys," she said. "Go ahead and make it all about you."

Rhys should have been kinder, he was aware of that, but he was worn down to the quick, every nerve exposed to the cold air of the study.

"How can I not? You said you wanted to hook up with strangers in front of my friends!"

When he was backed into a corner he could be cruel, and he saw Moira recoil from his words, but his blood was already ice in his veins.

"That's not what I said!" Moira snapped, mean as a hornet.

Above him, a hairline fracture cracked open the crown molding on the ceiling.

'They're just dreams," Moira went on. "And if I were you, I would watch what fights you wade into with me. I have been incredibly patient with you up until this point."

"Patient with what? What have I done to you?"

His breath coalesced around his mouth in an icy fog, and he would have given it more thought if he wasn't watching his wife sink in into herself. She was shivering and scowling with her arms strapped across her chest, and she refused to look him in the face.

"Do not play stupid with me; you don't have any ground to stand on."

"Are you implying something?"

She said nothing, just let his question hang in the air like an indictment. This, somehow, was worse than just accusing him of the unthinkable.

Rhys pressed his palms against the aged wood of his desk and leaned heavily against it. Rage and anxiety battled for dominance inside his chest, ticking up his heart rate.

"I have been absolutely, *painstakingly* faithful to you since our first date," he said, enunciating every word clearly. If he didn't focus on shaping the sounds, he would cry, or yell, both outcomes irrevocably disastrous. "How could you possibly think..." His throat felt like it was closing up, and he was positive the walls were straining forward to press the life out of him. He could hardly feel the tips of his fingers, they were so cold.

Moira sighed heavily, like she was the one being put on trial. "I didn't say you were unfaithful – God, don't do this to me, you're going to put yourself into a state."

"Then what *are* you saying?"

"I need you here with me, Rhys!" It sounded like some kind of dam had broken inside her, and now all the water was spilling out. "I need you here *now*, I can't handle the stress, I can't..."

Rhys forced himself to breathe, trying to maintain control of the situation. Moira was only getting more upset. He needed to ground her, he needed to fix this, he needed to *breathe*.

"What are you talking about?" Rhys asked.

She shook her head, the tendons in her neck taught. Then she turned and headed for the door.

"I don't want to talk about this right now. I just want to go to bed."

He darted around his desk, moving to catch her before she disappeared. An awful fear yawned up open inside him that if he let her leave the room now, she would never come back.

"Moira, please don't–"

The study door slammed shut with a crash, inches from Moira's face. She staggered backwards and Rhys caught her before she fell. She extradited herself from his grasp the moment she caught her balance.

Rhys was angry, angrier than he had been in a long time, and he didn't know what to do with all the fire under his skin. So he just stood there, feeling stupid and useless.

"I'm not sleeping with David," was what he managed in the end. As ludicrous as it felt, this *had* to be what this was about. Moira, after all, had cut ties with all her exes, the boys she had dated in high school and college. She had no problem burning bridges and moving on. But before Moira, Rhys had only *ever* dated David. As arrogant and self-destructive as David was, he was Rhys's strongest tie to the Boston occult scene, and Rhys had to see him at least once a week at Society meetings. Being civil, at least, was a foregone conclusion.

"I didn't say you were! It's not just about David. You put so much time into impressing everyone in the Society, and when they're around, you look right through me."

This gave Rhys pause, and if he had been thinking more clearly, he might have grasped onto this little bit of vulnerability as an opportunity to build a bridge. But they had been talking past each other for so long, building up resentment and disappointment, and now he couldn't find his way forward.

"I can't just make friends with the person in line at the grocery store like you can," Rhys went on, desperation rising in his voice. "I have never had an easy time with that. People look at you and they fall in love with you. The entire world falls over itself to get close to you, and I can barely get people to take me seriously. The Society is a lifeline to me, you should know that. David is an asshole, but he is my *friend*."

"How can you accuse me of being jealous about some spoiled little rich boy when you just blew up at me for having *dreams*? You're delusional, Rhys."

Moira was raising her voice, and for once in his life, Rhys – who detested shouting and would exit any conversation that deigned to include it – matched her volume.

"This is exactly why we can never talk about any of this! You get upset and I shut down and we go in circles!"

There was a distant rattling in the walls as plaster drifted down on them both from the cracks spreading across the ceiling.

"We're not doing this," she said, and her voice sounded wrung-out and dry. She braced her hands against the door and gave a defiant shove.

It didn't budge.

"It's locked," she croaked. A sheet of plaster and chunk of crown molding tumbled down from the ceiling, shattering near enough to Moira's feet that her toes were dusted with white. She let out a frustrated shriek. "I hate this house! We're going to die here in this damn study, with no one to find us for a week!"

The rattling was growing, shuffling books off the shelves and sending cobwebs drifting down from the ceiling corners.

"Why don't you just tell me what this is really about? We've been dancing around it for months, so you might as well just get it out there," he said. Rhys knew he should give up on this crusade and do what he was good for: clean the study, research their problem, try another spell. But the crack inside his heart was spreading to the rest of him, seeding tendrils of inadequacy and grief deeper than he could reach.

"You want to do couple's therapy now? Right now?"

"Tell me."

Rhys had a strong suspicion that he already knew what it was Moira had been keeping from him, and there was a cruel, masochistic part of him that wanted the satisfaction of hearing her say it.

"I don't..." Moira sucked in air through her nose as though physically pained. When she spoke again, her voice was soft, and that was somehow so much worse. "I don't know if we can do this, Rhys. We're just different people, and no matter how hard we try, we can never seem to build real trust with each other. Maybe we should take a step back and reevaluate. I just... I don't know. That's it."

Rhys pressed a hand to his chest as his heart seized. This was what he had been fearing since they exchanged vows, what kept him up at night while Moira dozed beside him, what he was so terrified of he couldn't even speak it aloud to himself.

A fatal misalignment, a gulf they simply could not cross.

Rhys's ears rang ceaselessly, pushing him towards the brink of saying something he could never take back.

He opened his mouth and took a breath, but then he realized something.

The rattling in the walls had stopped. And the room, while still intolerably cold, was no longer so frigid that his fingers ached.

"Sometimes, I wonder what my life would be like if we hadn't gotten married so young," Moira soldiered on, oblivious. Now that the Band-Aid had been ripped off her inner wound, the words came pouring out. "I know that makes me wicked, and I wish I could just be a better wife. But there's something wrong, inside me. I'm sorry it took me this long to tell you."

Rhys straightened and began to survey the room, his mind racing.

"Moira..."

"When I met you, I thought, there he is, that's the person I've been waiting for. But I see you with the other guys from the Society and it's like looking at a stranger. It's like I don't know you at all, and I wonder how well you know me, at the end of the day. There are parts of your inner world I just can't access, and there are things about me you'll never understand. I don't know if love is enough to make up for that. I really hope it is, Rhys. I pray for that every day. But I just don't know."

Striding with growing speed from one shelf to another, Rhys slid his hands across the books in his library. He stooped to rifle through the tomes thrown onto the floor, flipping open tables of contents before snapping them shut and dropping them again. Then he hurried over to Moira, the book he had been looking for balanced in his arms, and snagged her hand to tug her over towards his desk. Moira was so taken aback she stumbled after him obligingly. Her skin was warm under his touch, soft and alive.

Rhys placed the books down on his desk. Dog-eared pages fell open as his fingers scanned the lines of text.

"Please read this," he said.

"What?"

Rhys took a deep breath, turned to his wife, and clasped her shoulders in his hands.

He looked into her eyes, all that bottomless brown, and he did his best to find the right words. For once in his life, he hoped he could figure out the correct thing to say.

"The love is real, even if we haven't been tending it well for some time. And I hope every day it's enough too. But right now I'm asking you to trust me. Just one more time."

He plucked up a paperback from the mid-nineties that

had been loved nearly to death with highlights, post-
it-notes, and coffee stains. When he placed it in her
hands, he realized that he had never really shown her his
research up close before. He had always been too afraid
that it would bore her or irritate her magical sensibilities
in some way. Moira's practice was so dynamic and agile
that his, by contrast, felt dusty and rote. If any of her well-
planned spells faltered, she could improvise with herbs or
candles or crossroads dust to fix problems as they arose.
When one of Rhys's spells broke down, he broke down
too. He had been terrified she would lose all respect for
him when she realized he was tied to his books, bound by
his prayers, kept captive by every increasingly complex
ritual.

Now, as she balanced the book between her hands and
smoothed her fingertips down the crinkled page, Rhys felt a
vulnerable pang of hope.

"The section in blue," he said gently.

"'Though uncommon,'" Moira read aloud, "it is possible
under certain circumstances for a thoughtform to be created
passively, particularly in areas with high psychic traffic. Such
thoughtforms can be created from energy unwillingly lent by
one or more people and are generally less predictable than
those created with intention. They draw their animating
energy from highly charged emotions with a low vibrational
resonance, such as shame, anger, fear, or resentment.'"

Moira looked up at him, her face softening.

"So you're telling me that every time I got pissed at you,"
she said. "Or every time you kept a secret from me—"

"We were feeding it, yes. Programming it without
meaning to."

Her eyes darted from page to page, faster and faster as

the whole situation began to coalesce. She was always the clever one, responsive in the moments when he froze, and now, with all the pieces laid out before her, the puzzle came together neatly.

"That picture in the bedroom, and my lost necklace, the nightmares..."

Rhys nodded quickly, that hope in his chest growing wings.

"Yes, yes, exactly. It was sabotaging us with a hostile environment. If it feeds off negativity, it's incentivized to keep upping the ante on that negativity."

"Creating a perfect hateful ecosystem for itself," Moira muttered, wrinkling her nose. She placed the book back on the desk, closed the cover gently, and took a deep breath. She was centering herself, grounding in her body, and deciding what she wanted to say next.

Rhys held his breath through every agonizing second of quiet. Then, Moira breathed out through her nose and nodded.

"So this is what happens when you put two magicians in a house together, huh?" she said. "They didn't cover that in premarital counseling."

"No," Rhys said. "The priest was too busy cross-examining us about whether we were committing the sin of fellatio."

Nerves kept him from executing the joke smoothly, but Moira still snorted. Maybe their marriage wasn't down the drain after all. Maybe Moira didn't secretly resent him. Maybe he wasn't the perpetual martyr, and maybe there was still time to take responsibility for the role he had played in their predicament.

He swallowed hard and did his best to pry his heart open like a stubborn clam, revealing the tiny pearl of truth inside.

"Everything you said was right," he said. His fingers were shaking, so he clasped them tight in front of himself. He had to be brave, anxiety be damned. "We used to tell each other everything, and now it's like we can't be honest with each other anymore. When you reach out for me, I pull away because I don't know how to tell you what I'm feeling. I shut you out, and I try to shoulder all this stress and worry myself because that's how I was brought up, but that's not an excuse, and that's not fair to you. I let my own inadequacy rule me, and for that I'll always be sorry. But this explains why it targeted David but none of the other guys. He's a catalyst for negative emotions."

Moira gave a little shudder as she remembered the catastrophe in the magical circle.

"I was furious with him. I wished him ill. And maybe I did make the cupboards and the chandelier happen. But whatever that thing was that attacked him in the circle, I didn't tell it to."

"I know. That one was me."

Moira blinked, astonished, and Rhys rubbed the back of his neck.

"At least I think it was. That potshot he took at me really pissed me off, and I was kind of hoping something would put him in his place. David's the type to leverage the past against someone when he wants to make himself look better; it drives me insane."

"Well, there's no accounting for taste," Moira replied, her voice a little lighter, and Rhys actually laughed.

"Listen, Moira, I–"

He hit the floor before he could finish his sentence. The rug had been ripped out from under him and lay in a rippled heap beneath his throbbing back. Moira landed on top of him, kneeing him in the diaphragm, and now the ceiling was going in and out of focus above him as he wheezed for air.

Pulling herself to her feet, Moira spread her arms out and shouted to the room,

"This is getting *really old*!"

Her voice bounced off the rafters strangely and came back to her broken and sounding like laughter. Rhys had always felt safe in his study; it was his hideaway from the world. But now it felt cavernous and mocking.

Rhys stood and tossed a hand up to the ceiling, gesturing vaguely to the thoughtform, wherever it was.

"There's no use shouting at it. It's gotten strong enough to act on its own; it doesn't have to obey either of us anymore."

"No," Moira said, her barometer of tolerance well past critical mass. "I don't accept that. If we brought this thing to life, we can put it down."

"How?"

"Magic, of course."

"I wouldn't know where to start," he said. "I need time to research and cleanse the room–"

"Sometimes spontaneity is a witch's strongest advantage," Moira said, plucking up the salt and pepper shakers from the breakfast nook. Before the air between them had grown chilly and tense, she and Rhys would often sit there together and chat over Saturday coffee. "And weren't you just saying you're tired of shutting me out? Let me help for once."

The shutters started to bang wildly against the study windows, filling the room with a deafening racket. Moira pulled the stoppers out of the shakers with her teeth and poured a thin line of salt in a circle around where her husband stood.

"My momma calls these two the right and the left hand of God," she said, guiding him through her rationale. "Salt protects what is within and pepper drives back what is outside. No pair more powerful under the sun."

Moira worked with a precision Rhys typically associated with the best ceremonial sorcerers, pairing the salt with an unbroken line of pepper that hugged the curve perfectly. She was steady-handed despite the clamor, and even though Rhys felt sure the room was going to rise up to swallow them whole, he couldn't help but be impressed.

"We just had five magicians in this room and now we only have two," he said. "How are we supposed to wrestle it into the circle and bind it by ourselves?"

"In my tradition we lay down circles to keep things out, not call them in."

Rhys had to mentally jog to keep up with her line of reasoning, trying to suppress the panic he felt at doing anything remotely not by-the-book. She was making sense, her logic was sound, but anxiety was a spider crawling up Rhys's spine. The study was full of noises, rattles, creaks, and moans with no clear source of origin. It sounded as though the whole room was pacing around in a circle like a dog, half ready to settle down on them both.

"I know doing things the old-fashioned way makes you feel safe," Moira said, pausing his work long enough to fix him with her gaze. He knew that gaze, heavy and warm and full of promise. It was the first spell she had ever cast on him, the one that had burrowed under his skin and enchanted him with a love he never wanted to be free of. "But this whole mess is unorthodox to start with. You asked me to trust you a few minutes ago, and now I'm asking you to trust me back."

Rhys's eyes skittered between Moira and the darkest corners of the room. He swallowed hard. "What's your plan?"

She was up again, moving purposefully towards his desk. The rugs slipped under her feet and snapped their edges at her like snakes, but she bounded sure-footed on the groaning wood between them.

"Remember Dee?"

"Queen Elizabeth's court magician?"

"You used to tell me how Dee would perform magical operations while his assistant Kelley scried through a crystal. Dee couldn't hear or see the spirits that appeared, but Kelley could, and Dee recorded the messages they gave to Kelley."

"A decent plan, except we'd need a seer for that to work."

She was rummaging through his desk, turning over papers and yanking open drawers until she found what she was looking for. A perfectly clear crystal sphere the size of a softball, tucked away in a velvet-lined box. It had been given by the High Priest of Rhys's society to him as a welcome gift after he had been inducted, and Rhys, in his great shame, had hidden it away where no one could see. He was useless with a crystal ball, a scrying mirror, or any other kind of tool calibrated to help sorcerers see beyond the veil. Any power he had came from will and sweat and repetition, not through natural aptitude.

"I might not go around calling myself a psychic, but I can see well enough when it suits me," Moira said. "It's just not a gift I feel compelled to use often."

Rhys reached behind her and took up his dagger, lying sheathed next to his letters. Flame-bladed and set into an opal and oak handle, it was a gaudy holdover from his brief Wiccan phase, but he loved it to death. Rhys balanced it between his fingers, eyebrows knitted in intense thought.

"If we do this, you need to be my eyes and ears," he said, swallowing down the shame. Shame had no place here. Not in magic, and not in love. "I'll be blind in there, running the operation with nothing but you to guide me. We're going to have to work together."

"I can do my best. That I can promise."

Rhys looked to his wife, his lips parted to offer an apology, a declaration of devotion. Something. Anything.

Then, the light bulbs overhead buzzed valiantly one last time, before giving up the ghost and plunging the study into darkness.

"We're going to need candles," Rhys said. "Lots and lots of candles."

The High priestess

CHAPTER TEN

MOIRA

Truth be told, Moira had never scried a day in her life.

She had tried once, at a fourth-grade sleepover when the other girls urged her to pull the names of their future boyfriends out of the bathroom mirror. They had crowded into the little room, turned off all the lights, and pled with her, insisting that since her mother was a witch, Moira must be able to do the same tricks.

Moira had failed to produce the names, but not because she wasn't able to. She had looked into that mirror for only a few seconds before getting the crawling feeling something was looking back at her. When she had described the sensation to her mother the next morning, her mother had gripped the steering wheel of their Buick a little tighter and said, "If you can see them, sugar, they can see you. I don't want you trying anything like that again."

Moira never had.

Now, as she sat cross-legged in the middle of the circle of black and white with candles burning all around her, she wondered if her mother had been right to deter her from developing her gifts. Moira wasn't even sure she would be able to lay eyes on the thing when it came right down to it. She had always had a strong sense of intuition. She oftentimes picked up the phone to dial Rhys milliseconds before he rang her. She had even, on a few occasions, been able to see things that other people weren't able to: auras and black masses and whole people made of light.

It still didn't feel like enough.

Rhys stood over her with a straight spine, his unsheathed dagger in hand.

"The banishing ritual I'm going to try is an old standby. But I can't make promises about efficacy. I've tried it before on this thing on my own, with a 100 percent failure rate. I'm hoping that your energy will boost the spell's potency. God knows I feel better with you here, so that's a start."

Rhys touched a toe to the circle of salt at his feet.

"You're sure this will keep it out?" he asked. "We don't need any sigils or incantations?"

"My momma home-birthed me in a circle just like this, and I turned out fine. You want to keep something nasty away from something precious, salt and pepper will do the job."

"Good enough for me."

Slippery light licked the blade as he raised it above his head and pointed it to the ceiling. Moira watched, breathing shallow to keep from stirring the delicate atmosphere too much. She had never seen him at work before, not this close. By candlelight, his skin seemed to glow from the inside, and the ridges of veins on his arms stood out stark as riverbeds.

She was a little afraid of him then, the same way the

mangled body of Christ hanging above her head in his church had put a fear in her so quiet and wide it felt like love. She wanted to say it, that she loved him, but she wasn't sure if that word was allowed during his kinds of rituals. Instead, she said: "I'm ready."

Moira brought the crystal up like a spyglass to her eye as Rhys pulled his blade down into the center of the circle, drawing down whatever supernatural force he had been calling on. He touched the blade to his forehead and then to his belly, muttering words Moira couldn't understand in a low voice he had never had occasion to use with her. It sounded like kingliness, like silver hard as steel.

Around them, the shadows shifted. Moira had no other word for the way darkness slid past darkness, shuddering a bit as it woke. She wished sorely that she had time to meditate beforehand, or a cup of mugwort tea, or anything else to put her in a trance state suited to this kind of work.

"Nothing clear yet," she said. "But something's happening. Keep at it."

Rhys moved smoothly through his ritual, slicing a pentagram through the air on the eastern side of the circle. Outside the protective ring, darkness quaked, and as he dragged his dagger to the south, an inky shape began to form a few feet from the boundary of salt.

Moira pivoted on her knees, following the movement through her crystal. Her sight felt sluggish and muddied, and the fear that she was making the whole thing up threatened to snap her in its jaws and render her useless. But she breathed steadily and tracked the mass with an unwavering gaze.

"I've got eyes on it," she said.

Rhys completed his pentagrams at the west and north,

careful not to break the lines that connected the points, and as he did so, the creature drifted closer. It looked awfully person-shaped now, albeit like a person whose edges kept dissolving and forming again, eating up all the light in the room.

Then it turned its face on her, an awful blank face made of absolutely nothing at all, and Moira was suddenly nine years old again, scared shitless in the bathroom of a friend's double wide trailer.

For a moment she considered dropping the crystal ball and begging Rhys to help her break the door down so they could get a decent night's sleep in a motel. But then she remembered how small and ashamed she had felt after running away from that thing in the mirror. She remembered how her father had taught her how to throw punches in case boys or men ever grabbed at her, and how he always took her shoulder in his pin-stuck tailor's hand and praised her for not backing down from standing up for what was right.

Moira gritted her teeth against the fear and pushed through. "Three o'clock, Rhys, and getting closer. It's watching us. Whatever you're gonna do, do it quick."

Rhys pivoted, one palm up, the other brandishing the dagger.

"Little to the left," Moira said. "Yes, there! Dead in your sights."

Rhys breathed in deep and unleashed his magical expertise on the thoughtform. He addressed it in Latin, threatening it with the wrath of any spirits he had the power to command. Moira only knew a few words of Latin, but she could parse him compelling it in the name of the archangels, presumably to depart and never return.

Outside the circle, the tulpa simply cocked its head and regarded Rhys with curiosity.

"It..." Moira's heart fluttered faintly against her ribs, pitiful as a dying moth. "It's not working."

Rhys's shoulders fell. Unceremoniously, the tulpa began to drift in a lazy loop around the circle, fading bit by bit as it was absorbed back into the shadows of the house. In Moira's crystal, the darkness was still treacherous and full of life, but she could no longer make out any distinct shapes.

"I lost it," she said, her voice on the verge of breaking. "It's gone."

Rhys staggered back a pace. When Moira lowered the crystal, she saw what her husband saw.

A dim, quiet study in disarray.

Nothing more.

The dagger clattered to the ground next to Rhys's feet as he sank to the floorboards. He propped his elbows up on his knees and pressed the heels of his hands to his eyes, trying to keep the tears from coming.

"I'm sorry," Moira whispered.

Rhys just passed his hands over his face and shook his head, taking a shaky breath. He didn't speak for a long while, so long that Moira felt terrified he might never speak to her again. The grandfather clock ticked its reprieve, filling the silence so she didn't have to.

"You're not wicked," he said finally.

"What?"

"What you said earlier about yourself. You're not."

The flurry of complaints against Rhys's character she had lobbed at him came rushing back to her, and her face burned for shame.

"I'm sorry," she said. "I shouldn't have said those things to you. I should have never brought any of it up."

Rhys scrubbed his hand against his eyes, and it came back wet.

"No, that's exactly the problem. Don't you get it? We never bring anything up to each other. Too afraid of ruining a good thing. But not bringing it up just ends up ruining us anyway."

Moira drew her legs underneath herself. She tried to remember how to breathe, drawing the air into her lungs through the uncertainty and the pain.

"Is that it then? Are we ruined?"

"I don't want us to be," he said, his voice hollow. "But if we go on keeping things from each other, maybe."

"And what is it you've been keeping from me, Rhys McGowan?"

Rhys picked up his dagger and studied it. His tears had dried, but he still looked miserable. When he spoke, it was almost too soft to hear.

"I get... jealous sometimes. The florist calls you cara mia and gives you free bouquets. Your yoga teacher is always fawning over you. You can't go to a bar without people buying you drinks. You're like this... this light the world can't look away from."

"And what's wrong with that?" she said with a light laugh.

He winced a bit and Moira realized that, while she may be entitled to her exasperation, Rhys was exposing a point of pain that she should treat with dignity. It didn't make him right, and it didn't make her wrong, but she owed him that much, at least.

"I'm not saying you're doing anything bad," Rhys said.

"I know it isn't your fault, and it's a really wonderful thing; it's one of the things I love about you. But it makes me feel like… like you deserve better than me. I'm just… I feel like a black hole sometimes. I walk into a room and conversation dies. I open my mouth and all I can talk about is dead languages and demons. In case you haven't noticed, I'm a bit of a killjoy."

Moira shifted a little closer to him in the circle. "How long have you been keeping this to yourself?" she asked softly.

Rhys picked at his fingernails with his blade, studiously not meeting her eyes. "Day one or so."

"Rhys," Moira sighed.

"I just get embarrassed," he went on, yanking the words out of himself like he was pulling them up by the roots. "You deserve someone fun. Someone exciting. Someone with access to normal human emotions."

She settled her hand onto his knee. To her immense relief, he didn't pull away.

"Will you look at me, please?" she said.

Rhys met her eyes. They were dark as ever, troubled as a storm-tossed sea, but he was somehow lovely, even in his agony. Like a cold, clear night without any stars.

She loved him ferociously then, as strongly as ever.

"Why didn't you tell me?" she asked.

"I was afraid you'd think I was a controlling dick."

"Well, I was afraid you'd think I was a spoiled brat. So here we are."

They sat in silence for a moment, the warmth from the candles warding off the iciness of the room. Then Moira said,

"What I brought up earlier, about wanting to run off into the sunset by myself sometimes… It's not about you. You couldn't be any more of what I want, and I chose you for a reason. I just think, sometimes... Well, sometimes I worry that..." Her voice trailed off, and Rhys waited patiently, not pushing her until she was ready to speak. "I worry that there's this ache inside me for sensation and for love and for adventure that's too big for any one person to satisfy. And I feel so guilty for trapping someone as dedicated as you in a marriage with someone as flighty as me."

"If this is entrapment, I'll happily let you put the manacles on my wrists and the collar around my neck," Rhys said. "I married you because I love you just as you are, and because you make me better, and because I want to be the best thing that ever happened to you. Not because I wanted to put you into a cage and turn you into a Stepford wife."

"Thank you," Moira whispered.

"But the Society is also important to me, in a different way," he went on carefully. "I'm an ambitious person, and I'm not going to apologize for that. I want to advance in the ranks, I want a shot at the High Priesthood someday. I can't give that up. That's where I'm at right now. That's my best attempt at being honest."

"I know, baby. And I'm not going to ask you to give it up. But I'm not going to dim my shine to make you feel more comfortable, either. As much as I love you, I'd sooner die."

His fingers trailed tentatively upwards to cup her cheek.

"Is that it, then?" she asked, turning her face to press a kiss to his palm. "Is it over?"

Rhys ran his thumb over her cheek, lost in thought. Moira savored the sweetness, acutely aware that this might be one of the last times she could ever enjoy it. Tears gathered in her eyes, but she blinked them away. If this was how it ended, she wasn't going to go out crying.

Finally, Rhys spoke.

"Maybe we can meet in the middle. Maybe we can be good to each other without sacrificing ourselves. I'm not sure if it's possible. But I want to try."

A smile broke across Moira's face, and that's when the tears fell, spilling across Rhys's knuckles.

Suddenly, her back and shoulders were draped in a blanket of warmth. Moira curled and uncurled her fingers to get circulation into her thawing fingertips.

"Rhys, do you feel that?"

She snatched up the crystal ball and held it to her eye, peering into the black beyond the circle. There was a still a darkness there that moved of its own accord, but it was thinner now, less pervasive.

"What is it?" Rhys asked, leaning to spy through the glass as though it would do any good.

"Oh my God. Oh my God, I think I figured it out!" She discarded the crystal and took her husband's shoulders in her hands. "We couldn't banish it because there are still parts of us that want it here, the parts that keep the secrets it feeds on. Now its shrinking and–"

"The room's gotten warmer," Rhys breathed. He dropped his face into his hands with an immense weariness. "It was so easy, this whole time. We didn't even need magic."

Moira was breathless with excitement. She clambered up on her knees, taking his wrists in her hands and hauling him upright.

"Well, what else is there? There can't be that much, right? I'm ready to get my life back. What else haven't you told me?"

"Me?" Rhys demanded, feathers slightly ruffled. "What about you?"

Moira tried to speak but found she could not, as though there was something locked behind a door inside her she didn't have the key to. Rhys, for his part, looked like an animal that might bolt, and Moira saw clearly how they had gotten to this place. Both of them unwilling to lay their cards on the table first for fear that the other might not lay down theirs at all.

Moira, as it turns out, was braver than she thought.

"I worry that you think my magical practice is silly," she bit out. That was the last of it, the last damning confession that could either save or ruin them. "That it isn't as... I don't know. Legitimate as yours."

"Silly?" Rhys croaked. He let out a thin laugh. "You spend your day making people's lives better. How is that silly?"

"I don't know. It just seems like airhead new-age stuff compared to what you do. At least that's how it feels sometimes."

"You're proficient in more magical traditions than I will ever be, and you carry the torch of your ancestor's power passed straight down from your mother and grandmother. I never had someone to set me on my path, to teach me my traditions or give me advice. Hell, the closest thing I had to a mentor was David, and that was an absolute cock-up. If anything, I..."

He trailed off, withdrawing into himself once again, but Moira refused to let him slip away. She squeezed his hand, urging him forward.

"What is it?" she pressed.

"I worry that you don't think highly of *my* magical practice... That you think what I do is wrong."

"I don't understand the finer points of it, sure, and sometimes it scares me. But that's not the same as thinking it's wrong. We've talked this through plenty of times."

"I'm just never sure how well I express myself."

"Well," Moira said carefully. "You might have a better idea if you ever invited me to help with a ritual, or even watch. You hardly ever even talk about what you're researching to me."

Rhys's brows furrowed. "I just always assume people think what I study is boring. I guess I should have asked."

"I love hearing you talk about your work. Besides, you know I'm a fiend for learning new symbols and spells. I can't get enough of them."

"I'd love to have a better understanding of what you do as well, beyond the surface-level stuff. Especially astrology, if you're willing to share."

Rhys took Moira's face between his hands, moving his thumbs across the apples of her cheeks. He stared at her like she was revelation straight from the mouth of God, the same way he had looked at her in that crossroads, and on their wedding day.

"I wish I had half your skill," he said.

"Well then you'd better stick around," she teased, tracing his lips with her own. "Maybe you'll learn something."

Rhys kissed her, filling her with delicious warmth from the inside out. He ran his tongue along her lower lip, and Moira felt a shudder go through the room as the shadows relented in their restlessness and settled back into their proper places.

She could practically hear that dark, hateful thing breathing its last around them as her husband kissed her and kissed her, like they were already living in a world without end, like they could stay in this moment forever.

"I want you," Rhys said, honest as a desperate man's prayer, and Moira threaded her fingers through his hair.

"In the circle? I thought it wasn't proper conduct."

He dug his fingers into the softness of her hips and pulled her in close. "I don't care. Will you have me?"

"Any hour, any place."

She felt feather-light and half-drunk as she kissed him deeply, hands roaming across every inch of his chest.

This was her favorite kind of alchemy, the most potent form of magic.

"I don't ever want you to think I don't want you," Rhys said, trailing kisses down her neck. Rhys freed her from her blouse, exposing her breasts to the balmy air. "And no more vows of celibacy for the sake of magic, I promise."

Teeth sank into the juncture of her shoulder, just hard enough to make her giggle. Moira slid her hands down and unfastened his pants.

"Then show me how much you want me, sorcerer."

"Gladly, miss witch."

Moira found herself on the floor in the circle again, but the hardwood beneath her felt as though it had been baking in the sun. Moments later, she was being undressed by Rhys's deft scholar's fingers, her jeans discarded in a heap next to her blouse, her panties tugged unceremoniously over her ankles. She sloughed off Rhys's Oxford shirt and tugged off his chinos, and his clothes soon joined hers in the pile.

Rhys pulled Moira into his lap, and she wrapped her arms around him in an embrace tight as death. For a long while, Moira just held him in her arms, her hands smoothing his hair, her ankles hooked around his back. Rhys pressed his forehead to her breastbone, breathing in time with her heartbeat.

Then, a hum of pleasure escaped Moira's lips as Rhys slipped inside her and pressed a palm to the small of her back. The darkness shuddered, chastened by the sight, and dripped off their bodies as smoothly as water.

The air swirled about them warm and kind when Rhys pressed his mouth to her throat. With every roll of her hips the shadows receded further into their corners, and with every pulse of his fingertips against her spine, the temperature in the room rose.

When her thighs trembled as she approached her climax, no curios rattled, no portraits wept. The house was blissfully silent save for her breathless giggles and Rhys's encouraging murmurs.

Moira crested and broke against Rhys like a wave, and every light in the house came on.

The Chariot   High priestess

ACKNOWLEDGMENTS

The resurrection of this book, first independently published seven years ago when I knew very little about what I was doing besides how much I loved telling stories, has been wonderful to witness. It's so rare that an author gets to revisit any work at all, especially something so personal and beloved, and I feel incredibly blessed to have been given the opportunity to rewrite and republish this book.

I have to thank those who were there in the early days, the friends who helped me edit the novella for its original publication, and those who arrived later to help me make it even better, including the entire Angry Robot team. However, I must especially thank those who have been here the whole time. Ellie and Kit: I would be nowhere without either of you. Thank you both for ceaselessly enriching my life in irreplaceable ways (and for fishing me out of every plot hole I fall into).

Thank you to Lena, the original cover artist, and to Eleonor, the phenomenal illustrator of the new and improved edition, and to Alice, designer extraordinaire. Thank you to each and every bookseller who has gushed about this series to patrons, and to every blogger, TikTokker, and bookstagrammer who has passed along a good word to their followers.

Finally, thank you to the readers who have been here since I was posting on Tumblr about a ceremonial magician and a tarot witch who fell in love. There are many of you who have kept the candle burning for my work in ways I'll never even fully understand, and for that I am grateful from the bottom of my heart. Thanks for being here, and thanks for giving me a second shot at making this book stronger, kinder, and more authentically me.

May love and magic always find you.

THE CHARIOT

Chariots have speed and energy, so can carry you forward, often very quickly. They can also take you upwards into heaven, as we see in Ezekiel's vision from the Old Testament. The Chariot image usually faces you head-on, so it can be cocky and ostentatious, but many of us need some of that confidence. Still, it's not always straightforward: in many card iterations, the Chariot is drawn by the mysterious figure of the Sphinxes. Sphinxes are well-known for their riddles, so your forward motion won't necessarily be instantaneous or easy. Chariots were included in a victory parade, especially in Ancient Greece and Rome, and they are useful in battle.

The Chariot is a card of success.

The High priestess

THE HIGH PRIESTESS

The High Priestess is full of mysterious imagery. She conveys an inner power – not masculine might or anything that overpowers – but energy in deep currents and dark places. She is an initiator, and she sits in front of a veil emblazoned with pomegranates which are the fruit of Persephone, the Greek goddess who spends six months of the year in the Underworld. She has transcended the mysteries of life and death. She is the patron saint of "I can't explain why" when we try to explore our motivations. She sits between the black and the white pillars of the Temple and is quite comfortable holding that space in between. Finally, behind the veil – behind everything – are the waters of the unconscious.

With her, you will go deep, find out something surprising and learn from your intuition and your instincts.

We are Angry Robot, your favourite independent, genre-fluid publisher, bringing you the very best in sci-fi, fantasy, horror and everything in between!

Check out our website at www.angryrobotbooks.com to see our entire catalogue.

Follow us on social media:

Twitter @angryrobotbooks
Instagram @angryrobotbooks
TikTok @angryrobotbooks

Sign up to our mailing list now: